Cursed Magic

A Novella

STEVE PANTAZIS

ISBN: 978-1-7354242-0-0

Written by Steve Pantazis

Cover illustration: Rebecacovers

Published by SP Books

To my wife, my love, my one and only

BONUS JUST FOR YOU

You're awesome! As a heartfelt thank you, you can get a **FREE eBook** just by signing up for Steve's newsletter:
https://www.stevepantazis.com/join2

CONTENTS

ACKNOWLEDGEMENTS

This book shines because of the sharp eyes, astute minds and brilliant suggestions from a talented group of writer-extraordinaire friends. A heartfelt thanks goes out to them for their time and generosity.

FOREWORD

EPIC FANTASY takes many forms, but at its core, it's about larger-than-life stories set in realms of wonder. Dragons, wizards, heroes, villains, magic and mighty battles are just a few things we know and love as fans of the genre. I was first introduced to fantasy when I was in second grade. I had enough allowance money to buy one book at the school fair. As soon as I picked up the paperback copy of THE HOBBIT, I knew it was for me.

I gobbled up the novel, then began writing my own fantastic tales. Stories of elves, dwarves and trolls. Quests filled with peril and excitement. The more I read, the more I wrote. I fell in love with fantasy, and I've been in love ever since.

Now that I'm grown up (sort of), I get to share my stories with the world. The fact you have this book in your hands is a testament to a dream come true.

CURSED MAGIC is about the hero's journey, but of the unlikely hero. I wrote it to be a fun piece, but as I got into the characters, conflict and stakes, I realized it was going to be much more.

In other words, it has all the feels.

Thank you for choosing CURSED MAGIC.

I hope it recaptures the joy of childhood adventures as you let your imagination soar.

CURSED MAGIC

CURSES AND MORE CURSES!

When the mayor of Saplinger asked for an arcanist to handle a "small lizard problem" in his town, I assumed it would be a spitster, wyvernette or one of those pesky horned minidrakes. But a basilisk? A great hulking, winged beast with the foulest inclination and claws the size of barn nails?

Heavens no!

Yet here I am, drenched by the rain and muddied below the waist, standing in a tavern stinking of sodden hay, listening as the mayor goes on and on about the disappearance of his livestock while the frightened townsfolk bob their heads in agreement.

Of course, I have to ask the mayor the obvious question.

"How can you be sure it's a basilisk? It very well could be something else. A pack of wolves maybe, or raiders from the Gray

Hills, or—"

"Haven't you been listening to me, mage? It's a basilisk. I'd stake my life on it. Angus, show him."

A weepy old man brings a tattered book to me with a page open showing a hand-drawn sketch of a creature with large wings, a barbed, coiled tail, and, I daresay, a smirk on its face.

"It's him," he says. "I've seen him with my own eyes. Took my goats and my chickens, too. He had a great big head, lots of scales, shaggy wings. And teeth. Those teeth!"

"I've seen him, too," an aged woman says. "He stole my only cow, my poor Bertha. Snatched her up in the early morn."

"And my ma's pigs," ventures a sturdy young lad.

"And our donkey," someone else says.

"And my sheep."

"He'll come for the children next! What will we do then?"

The room fills with anxious commotion. The aroma of meat stew from the kitchen reminds me that I haven't eaten a hot meal in weeks while on the road with my tired horse and rickety cart.

The mayor quiets down his people. Then he asks, "Do you believe us now, mage?"

The taproom's a field of blinking eyes and uncertain faces, everyone looking at me. What can I say but yes? "I do."

"We don't have much coin, but we've scraped together what we can." The mayor opens the drawstrings of a purse and shakes the coins inside so I can see them. They jingle their lovely tune. Thirty silver marks, as promised in the urgent letter I'd received. Enough to keep me and my trusty steed fed for a couple of months. Hardly anything by arcanist standards, and certainly not a prize worthy of such risk.

Which is why the mayor chose me.

You don't pay so little for a quality arcanist; you pay it when you're desperate, when you wipe the pig slop away and see what's left at the bottom of the trough. That slimy residue is where I dwell.

"Slay the beast and the purse is yours," he says.

Hearty nods all around. They believe I'm suited for the job. How wrong they are. But for thirty marks . . .

"What do you say, mage? Will you use your great magic to help us?"

This is the point where my peers would fall to the ground laughing. Great magic? Me? Never have the two been spoken in the same breath.

Faulty magic? Yes. Terrible magic? Absolutely! But great magic?

Never!

Why, Ellis, do you doubt your abilities, you might ask?

A most excellent question.

I'm cursed, you see.

Imagine a young boy . . . a bright child with a gleam in his eye and hope in his heart. His father is a merchant, his mother a seamstress for a duchess, his older brother a knight in the Queen's Guard. This young lad is fed, clothed, schooled, and given the opportunity to attend the prestigious Arcanist University in the capital city of Ravenmore, the most sought-after opportunity for aspiring magic casters. It's during his first quarter that a miscalculation in Spell Weaving results in shattering the stained-glass window of the University chapel. Then a blunder in Alchemy that causes a violent explosion. Then a Potion Making accident. Wand Crafting incident. Elemental Divination disaster. Spirit Mediation catastrophe. And then an error in Pyrotechnics that sets fire to the main library, salvaged by a quick-thinking professor.

And finally . . .

Expulsion.

Only after paying a soothsayer to uncover the mystery of his disastrous quandary does he uncover the truth:

He's cursed.

Not a little cursed. Not marginally cursed.

Completely cursed!

As in cursed so deeply that it can never be undone. Born that way, the soothsayer had said, and destined to live out his days that way.

You've heard correctly: the lad's as cursed as cursed can be.

Want to apply a magical solution to deal with nasty vermin? Good luck. An invocation to reverse the jinx laid upon you by a spiteful witch? Keep your fingers crossed. A spell to protect your land and her people against a violent and ruthless horde of berserkers? Don't even think about it!

Thus life takes young Ellis on a shameful path as an uncertified arcanist only the poor can afford and the despondent dare consider, even now at the ripe old age of sixty-two.

People like the good townsfolk of Saplinger.

"I have a couple of conditions," I say to the mayor, realizing he isn't a very friendly fellow by the way his lip curls like a rabid dog frothing at the mouth. "One, a hot bath. Two, a hot meal. Three, a room to sleep. And four, a guide to accompany me into the forest. Someone who knows their way and someone who won't get us killed."

The mayor shrivels his nose. "That's four conditions, not two." Then he says, "I'll agree to the first three. As for the fourth, you're on your own. I'll not send my people into that anathema of a forest, unless someone wants to volunteer."

It's as if the entire tavern shrinks back.

I can't blame them. Who would be foolish enough to go with me? They're afraid, scared for their lives, and especially for the lives of their children. Perhaps they're cowards, and rightfully so. Cowards live, after all. But volunteers? Best of luck to the poor sap that joins the cursed arcanist. Good luck to him indeed! It reminds me of the time—

"I'll do it."

We all look to the back of the tavern, following the sound of a young lady's voice. There's a teenage girl standing along the wall. She's maybe sixteen or seventeen, a skinny urchin with smudged cheeks and threadbare clothes. I'm not the only one who doubts my ears. It's as if the words were conjured from thin air, not her.

"I'll do it," she says again, putting to rest any doubts.

I'm happy to accept this most unlikely volunteer, but the mayor seems to disagree. He wags a finger at the girl. "Absolutely not. I forbid it." Then to me, he says, "Forgive my niece, Sera.

She's, how should we say, enthusiastic at times."

"It's not enthusiasm, Uncle. It's called courage." Sera's voice matches her fire-red hair. The townsfolk part to allow her through. "I know the forest better than anyone. I can follow the trails and track that horrid beast to his lair. Who else here would do it? You, Uncle? Any of you?" She points at the others, who shrink back even farther.

"Sera, please—"

"I said I'll take him, and that's that."

The room falls silent. The air is so still, I could slice it with a farmer's scythe.

I like Sera's indomitable spirit. It reminds me of myself at her age, believing I could achieve anything. Of course, courage has its downside, but I keep that to myself.

I speak up, as her uncle seems to have lost his tongue. "Then it's settled. We head out at first light."

* * *

THE FOREST AROUND SAPLINGER IS THICK, laden with mist in a dawn that portends more clouds and possibly rain, and hopefully not our demise.

Sera and I lead our horses between the thick boughs as a woodpecker welcomes our arrival with its hammering song, lost in the shroud of fog above us. We travel along a streambed that burbles over roots and rocks as the musky-sweet scent of the decomposing forest sweeps over us. Belly full and body clean, I've not felt this good in weeks, although the gnawing dread of the task ahead has me gripping my reins tightly. My horse, Sienne, feels it too, her withers shaking. I try to soothe her with gentle talk.

"Now, now, it'll be all right. Just a little farther."

Sera's horse Ranger is a hand shorter and even more skittish than mine, but Sera's better than I am with the reins. She's curious, too, stealing glances at me, as if trying to figure out if I'm a fraud.

"Why don't you say what's on your mind?"

She acts as if I've caught her taking coins from the queen's coffers. "It's nothing really, only that . . ."

"Yes?"

"Is it true you toppled Duke Arold's keep with a windkeeper spell?"

So, there it is: my inglorious reputation preceding me. "Yes, it's true. And how did you come across this lovely piece of history, pray tell?"

Her cheeks flush a healthy apple color. "My uncle told me about it. Not the spell. I learned about that elsewise. I'm sorry, I didn't mean to . . . impose."

"That's quite all right. Most people know nothing about the spell, only that I knocked down the keep while trying to defend it against barbarians. The duke was deeply in debt to the crown, so he hired me, imagining he was getting the bargain of a lifetime. I thank the gods no one got killed. I do recall that my incompetence drove the barbarians away, though. They're a superstitious lot, you know." I chuckle, alone finding humor in the tragedy. "You seem keen on spells."

She looks down at her thin fingers. "I want to learn magic someday."

Now I understand why she volunteered, poor girl. "I'm not looking for an apprentice, if that's what you think."

"Of course not. I would never assume that." She fidgets with her reins. Of course she assumed that. I wait for her to ask me if it's all right to turn around, to be done with this silly and dangerous business, but she says nothing and continues alongside me.

"Why magic? Why not some other calling? Magic is often more troublesome than it's worth. Take that from someone who's an expert on the matter."

She looks at me more confidently now. "I've loved magic my whole life. It started when my mum told me stories as a young girl. I know my destiny lies outside Saplinger. Saplinger is for girls who dream of milking sheep and marrying the boy with the crooked teeth from over the hill. My mum and da are both dead. I have no sisters, no brothers. I'm eighteen now. There's nothing to keep me here, save my uncle, who would see me married off and kept barefoot and stupid. I'm of age now. I plan to leave for Ravenmore in the spring, with or without his approval. I've heard there's a shortage of arcanists. If I were of a better class, I might apply to the University. I can read and write, you know."

She's spirited and ambitious, I'll give her that. Naïve, of course, but bold as well. "Ravenmore is not for the faint of heart. There are plenty of charlatans who would pull you into their disgraceful business of peddling potions and false remedies. Maybe you can find someone to apprentice you. Better yet, go to the mage's guild and ask for a reputable arcanist. Although I wouldn't give up on attending the University. I attended, and look how I turned out."

What should earn me a smile gets a frown instead.

"Did I say something wrong?"

"No, but . . ." She pauses. "I've been told the University has been closed and the arcanists are gone."

"Closed? As in shut down? Impossible! Where did you hear that nonsense?"

Sienne's ears pin forward stiffly and she flares her nostrils. I smell it too: a foul odor, like rotten meat. We'll resume our chat when the time is right.

Sera slows her steed to a halt. "We should go on foot from here. The horses are spooked."

We tie off our horses and journey into the dank stillness. The woods are strangely quiet in the gloom, with patches of mist obscuring the canopies above.

Sera takes the lead. With each step, the odor grows stronger. We stop every so often so she can take stock of our surroundings. A freshly felled tree, broken branches, a disturbance that had created a trail through decaying leaves. Sera's a waif of a lass, pale-skinned with a dash of freckles, woefully thin, but strong in carriage. Her eyes are filled with determination. I couldn't have asked for a better companion.

"May I ask you something?" she says on one of our stops. "How do you plan to defeat this creature?"

Ah, yes, that. What does a great magician do against a fearsome basilisk?

"The most important factor in defeating a basilisk is the element of surprise. They slumber during the day, waking at dusk to feed. If we can ambush the beast while it sleeps, we can defeat it. I have an incantation or two in mind. And this." I pull out a wand strapped beneath my cloak. It's made of wood from the rare Quellen tree. Any arcanist worth his salt owns at least one. Even those that aren't any good.

"One more thing, and this is important: don't look the creature in the eye. Doing so is bad. Like you're dead kind of bad, understood?"

Sera pulls a dagger from her belt. "I have this." It's about as effective against a basilisk as a sword against a giant gray cougar.

"Right." I motion and we continue forward.

It's late afternoon when we arrive at a deep bowl in the forest, a depression that leaves a gaping cavern beneath the exposed roots of a tall, gnarled tree. The overpowering stench of death seeps from the opening. It looks like the smile of a halfwit gone mad. Sera points at the hole. We crouch behind the tree leaning over the edge of the bowl.

I keep my voice to a whisper. "The beast is in there, asleep. Listen." The basilisk's snore comes out as a rumble, like distant thunder. Gods, it must be huge.

"Should we go in after him?"

"In there? Have you lost your mind?"

"But you said—"

"I know what I said. These beasts have a keen sense of smell, keener than even a bear. They hunt by scent. If we go in, it'll smell us and wake, and that'll be the end of us."

"Don't you think you should have mentioned that fact earlier?"

"You're the one who wanted to 'track that horrid beast to his lair,' armed with your mighty blade no less. And stop saying 'he.' It very well could be a 'she.'"

"Fine. 'It' then. What do we do?"

"Our best chance is to stay where we are and ambush it after it rouses. We'll catch it unawares, drugged with the lingering effects of sleep."

"We're to wait behind a tree? That's your plan?"

I tug on my beard. The girl has a point. We have scant cover, with one chance to strike, and strike true. Even an all-powerful magus would hesitate if in our position. What I wouldn't give for a keg of highly-combustible fire oil right now. Set it aflame, roll it down the hole, and hope the explosion does the trick.

"We need to distract the beast. Lure it out, occupy its attention, and subdue it. The pertinent question is, how?"

Of course, these are things I should have considered *before* our outing. Planning, I'll admit, has never been one of my strong suits.

Sera's face brightens. She's grinning ear to ear. "I have an idea that might work."

* * *

THERE ARE GREAT IDEAS, there are foolish ideas, and then there are ideas that are downright terrible.

Sera's idea falls in the latter category.

"This is a terrible idea," I whisper.

"Hush, you'll scare the pigs."

That's right: we're hunkered down in the shadows of an empty barn by the pigpen, kneeling among bits of hay and the stink of dung. Sera's brilliant idea to lure the beast to us is to lie in wait on Ilma Millins' scratch of a ranch and use one of her sows as bait. Sera isolated the fattest sow from the others, presently standing chained to a stake pounded into a tree stump under the open, moonlit sky. A good smearing of chicken blood on its flank completes the trap, and now we wait.

The mayor wasn't too keen on bringing trouble his way, but Ilma was of a different mindset.

"Save me pigs, please, wizard. If I have to sacrifice poor Harriet, so be it."

"Now, now," I'd said. "We'll do our best to save Harriet."

In truth, I'm more worried about us than Harriet.

The cold air seeps into my hair as the moon arcs overhead. I start to nod off when Sera bumps me. Quietly she says, "Listen."

I hear the chirp of crickets, the snort of restless pigs, maybe an owl in the distance. There's nothing out of the ordinary—

—except there is.

I catch a faint *whoomp* sound. It grows louder, like someone's beating a rug with a stick.

Not the beating of a rug, I realize, but the flap of wings. Huge wings!

I come to my feet. "Get ready."

We position ourselves just inside the open barn doors and peek out.

Harriet snorts and tugs at her chain, growing frantic and squealing. I hear the other pigs rustling in their pen, bunching together and squealing too.

"There!" I point to the shadow flying across the moon.

The basilisk circles overhead, flapping its ragged wings with a heavy *whoomp*. It looks small from here, a black silhouette, but it's high up and I know better.

I prepare my wand and incantation. Please let me get this right. Please, please, please.

A piercing shriek makes the hairs on the back of my neck stand on end, and the creature dives toward the ranch.

It grows larger as it hurtles to the earth, wings pinned back, wretchedly graceful in its descent. It seems like it's going for poor Harriet, but then it veers slightly and plummets in the direction of the pen. Like a hawk, it draws its wings back and extends its greedy talons. I step out from my cover and point my wand.

"Hericulus!"

The pen's fencing cracks down the middle with a loud split and the rails crash to the ground.

Curses, I missed!

Pigs bolt for the opening in a panic, but not before the basilisk swoops and grabs onto the back of one with a monstrous talon. The pig struggles furiously, dragged squealing through the mud as the basilisk flaps its wings, flinging mud in my face.

Before I can conjure the incantation from my throat, Sera is out in front of me running toward the pen. What in the blazes is she doing?

"Sera, no!"

The pigs scatter toward us. Sera jumps out of the way just in time, but then the basilisk is aloft, squealing prize in its claws, and my advantage is lost. Prey grasped neatly, it wheels north.

"It's headed toward the town!" Sera cries.

"Follow it!"

We ride our horses from Ilma's ranch at a fast gallop, using the moonlight to guide us. The basilisk *whoomps* ahead. Just as it seems that it will continue on toward its lair in the forest, it circles back over the town square. It's seeking a perch.

Sera, a couple lengths ahead, calls back to me. "The chapel! It's going for the chapel!"

We burst into town. Not a soul is out, the buildings lit up sharply by the moon. I pick up the screech of the basilisk to the east. My horse skids to a halt, Sera's too. They neigh, frightened, about to rear up and toss us off.

Sera and I dismount and rush toward the chapel.

The basilisk has landed on the pitched roof by the steeple, pig thrashing in its clutches. Shingles cascade off as the beast seeks purchase. It tears into the steeple with open jaws, splintering wood and ripping off chunks at a time. It's trying to go inside, where it can slaughter the pig and feast.

Chilled sweat drips from my brow and my legs ache like they've never ached before. If the basilisk decides to abandon the chapel, we'll lose our chance.

The tip of my wand glows bright as we close in on the chapel. I'm going to catch it off guard and—

A bloodcurdling screech shocks my ears. I stop, Sera as well.

Both of us are gasping to catch our breath. The basilisk cranes its neck as if it's detected our presence. It sniffs the air with its large, flaring nostrils. It then opens its talons, and the helpless pig slides off the roof squealing. The hapless pig lands on the ground with a dreadful splat and goes still. Talons gripping the roof, the basilisk lifts its head higher as it spreads its ragged wings. It's bigger than I imagined, frighteningly huge, more dragon than drake.

Gods!

I motion for Sera to take cover, and we drop behind the stone wall of the town's well, panting and perspiring.

"Don't look at its eyes," I say.

"It's going to come for us."

"I know!"

I risk a peek. The basilisk is leaning forward in our direction. It knows we're here, and it's ready to spring.

I would have expected to die falling off my horse, not get eaten alive or drop dead from a basilisk's gaze. But that's exactly what's about to happen to me.

My wand's gone dark. I can't think. I can't—

"Do something!" Sera says.

The one incantation—the only incantation I can think of— leaves my lips.

"*Magnum eruptus!*"

The ground shakes all around me. A big belch of earth catapults me upward while the earsplitting crack of wood assaults my ears. I hit the ground a moment later, the buildings creaking, splintering and crashing around me in a deafening avalanche of sound.

The world blacks out an instant later.

* * *

"OVER HERE!"

I cough up dirt as a pair of hands rolls me onto my back.

The sunlight, so devastatingly bright, stings my eyes as I blink into consciousness. Is this the afterlife? Have the gods come to take me through the gates of the Eternal Kingdom, to rejoice in all the splendor of its magnificent glory?

No. None of that.

A wrinkled face looks down at me. "He's alive."

Wisps of cloud drift in an unblocked vista of the sky. On the periphery, I catch a ring of broken timbers, piles of thatching, part of a window shutter. Gods, what have I done?

"Sera?" I cough again, throat dry as a husk.

A waterskin presses against my lips, and I suckle deeply, drawing in water to rinse my parched throat and clear my foggy mind.

I'm helped into a sitting position. Ash and earth fall from my person. I smell charred wood. As my eyes adjust, the evidence of my handiwork smolders all around me.

I stumble to my feet and the world spins. I wait for it to stop.

Where's Sera?

I catch the mayor of Saplinger and two other townsfolk attending to her. She's sooty from head to foot, but unharmed, thankfully.

"Sera!"

She sees me and smiles. "Ellis."

"Are you all right?" Then I remember the last moment before

I blacked out. "The basilisk!"

"Dead," Sera says.

"Are you sure?"

The mayor points to the demolished chapel, where a barbed tail pokes out from between the collapsed timbers. He's not pleased to see me, not pleased at all. He stalks over to me, fists bunched. "Do you know what you've done here, mage? You've destroyed my town! I should have you arrested right now!"

"Uncle, he killed the beast. He saved us!"

"You call this saving us?" The mayor is mad, and I don't blame him. About twenty of the residents have gathered around us, their faces a forest of stupefied looks, while others search through the rubble. I've made a mess. The whole town is a wreck.

Sera continues her defense in my favor. "Is anyone dead? No, Uncle. But if you arrest him, you'll have to arrest me too."

The mayor doesn't seem to recognize his brash niece. His face has a twinge of purple. Anger? Embarrassment?

He shakes a finger at me. "Don't think this is over."

Definitely anger.

"I believe this is yours." Sera hands me my wand.

I run my finger over the wood. It's knobby like knuckles, a beautiful imperfection, one that I've come to know and love. "I've missed you," I whisper to the wand. Sera is smiling. "What?"

"Nothing," she says.

"Arcanists do speak to their wands, you know. They're like children to us." It sounds silly, even to my own ears, but Sera respects me enough not to laugh at me. "In case you were wondering, this is Isabella. Yes, we name them, too."

"I see."

The rush of hooves fills the air, cutting me off from making an even bigger fool of myself. We all turn our heads to witness the arrival of a dozen riders carrying the standard of the queen, a purple device with white stripes across a shield and a griffin clutching a spear within its talons. They're soldiers from the Queen's Guard. Why would they be here? Certainly not at the mayor's behest. Could they have found out about the basilisk?

The lead rider dismounts and strides over to us. He's outfitted in breast and backplates, greaves and shin guards, his helm crested in a plume of purple and red. He eyes the devastation with borderline interest.

The mayor bows low to the ground. "Sire, Mayor Dallen at your service."

"Lord Henneth," the man says. He's not used to dealing with low folk, I can tell by the twist of his aristocratic lip.

"We're in a bit of a crisis," the mayor says. "So I hope you don't mind—"

"I do mind. I'm told there's an arcanist among you. Where is he?"

I raise my hand. It's covered in soot and ash like the rest of me.

The lord furrows his brow, as one might expect when observing someone who looks like he just climbed down a chimney. "Heronium Ellis Blackfoot?"

"It's Whitefoot, actually."

"By decree of Queen Esmerelda the Kind, you are hereby summoned to appear before Her Majesty at once."

The queen wants to see me? Me, the least significant person in the kingdom? Could word of the basilisk's death have reached her ear? Impossible! The capital city of Ravenmore is a good two days' ride on horseback. "I'm sorry, did you say summoned before the queen?"

"I did."

"But why?

"I'm not at liberty to say. It's a matter of grave importance, and secrecy is a must."

If I was baffled before, I'm befuddled now. "But I'm . . . I'm a nobody."

"Are you not Ellis the Arcanist, son of Gelvin, practitioner of the magical arts, and dutiful servant of the crown?"

Well, when you put it that way . . .

I bow my head. Gray ash falls from my hair. "Ellis Whitefoot at your service."

"Gather your belongings. We are to depart at once."

The mayor interjects. "Lord Henneth, this man is responsible for the calamity you see before you. Reparations must be made before I release him. He's violated his contract with the good people of Salinger. He must be held accountable."

The lord sighs. "What contract?"

"He was hired to slay a basilisk. He's killed the beast, yes, but destroyed my town in the process."

"Then he's fulfilled his obligation of slaying the beast, yes?"

The mayor's cheeks puff up. "Does this look like fulfilling one's obligation?"

"Mayor Dallen, this man is under order to appear before the queen. If you have objection to this, then I suggest you take it up with the crown. Or would you prefer to press the matter further and receive judgment on the spot?"

The mayor, utterly flushed and flustered, bows in deference. "Of course not, milord."

"Then I bid you good day. Mage, say your goodbyes and let us be on our way."

I look at the ash swaddling my body. I suppose a dunk in the river en route to the capital could take care of it.

"I have a condition."

Lord Henneth tilts his head to the side, more irritated than ever. "And what is that?"

"She goes with me." I point to Sera, whose red hair is fifteen shades of ash.

Lord Henneth blinks a few times, as if he's stepped into a dark fairytale. "Who's she?"

I take another noble bow, this one deeper. "Why, my apprentice, Sera of Saplinger."

* * *

IT'S BEEN YEARS since I've set foot in the capital. Purple pennants snap in the wind high above the round citadel whose sheer walls blend with the bleached cliffs that tumble into the blue-gray Narrows below. Ravenmore sits strategically at the tip of an isthmus that separates the Narrows from the tributary of the Silver

River, giving the Kingdom of Warren the advantage on sea and land. I take in the wonder through Sera as her eyes travel from the citadel to the barges unloading their goods to the cutters crossing the water to the mighty warships docked in the expansive, sickle-shaped bay.

"It's like nothing I've seen," she says. "It's so . . ."

"Noisy?"

"I was going to say big. It's huge! I keep wanting to pinch myself."

"It'll get old soon enough, trust me."

"You're no fun. Tell me what to expect. Have you ever seen the queen? Have you been to court?"

"No and no. Succinctly put, I attended the University as a lad, screwed up royally, and was ousted before the year was up. I spent most of the time with my nose buried in books, scrolls and dusty tomes. That, and getting laughed at by my classmates. I couldn't tell you what to expect at court, much less what to see in the city, although I've visited the Arcanist Guild a number of times on business, and mostly on poor terms. My time here was—how can I phrase it?—a quagmire wrapped in a blanket of disappointment."

Sera's shoulders sag. I've let her down. I should have made something up about my time in the capital, but the truth always seems to work its way out of my mouth.

"That said, it would be an honor to show you around the University. I have a dear friend who still works in the library I almost burned down. Borgess Copperton. He knew everybody's business—all of the professors and my fellow students—and he befriended many arcanists, although he never became one himself, sadly. He dabbled in the craft in secret, was quite talented from what I remember. He can regale you with tall tales of my woes as he gives you the finest tour you've ever experienced." Then I recall what Sera had told me in the forest about the preposterous notion that the University had shut down. "The University is open for business, I assure you. As my mother would say, 'Never put your trust in rumors.'"

That brings out a guarded smile. It's good enough for me.

We arrive at the citadel's gate where more members of the Queen's Guard await us by the raised portcullis. I straighten my back in preparation for our royal encounter.

"Sera of Saplinger," I say proudly, "it's time to meet your queen."

* * *

THE QUEEN'S COURT is a stiff affair of formality, with her retinue of advisers, nobles and sycophants gathered around her in a large audience chamber, smelling of perfume and abhorrently-scented lace. Sera and I are down on one knee before the gilded throne, heads dipped, while Lord Henneth stands beside us with his helm in hand, pressed ceremoniously against his chest.

"You may rise."

I've always imagined the queen to be a regal woman of incalculable beauty and divine proportion, sculpted by the gods for us mortals to throw ourselves before her dainty feet.

It so happens the queen is as soft as the cushions of her throne, nowhere near as dainty as I pictured, wrapped in a bounty of expensive samite barely able to contain her generous figure. Her hair is a curtain of rust-colored ringlets, speckled with white and draped to her shoulders, matching the rouge in her plump cheeks and white makeup caked elsewhere on her face. If her court sees what I see, their fabricated smiles don't reveal it. Still, she's my queen. On one side of her throne stands a man in an ornate toga with a powdered face and soft, pampered hands, and on the other side a rough man with pockmarked skin and epaulettes over a worn breastplate. Her chief arcanist, Ruel Bisset—Ruel the Bold as he is best known—is glaringly absent. I had looked forward to seeing the old chap.

"Ellis Whitefoot, do you know why you're here?" There's an unexpected shrillness to the queen's voice, magnified in the grand chamber. Is anyone flinching? No, just me?

"I do not, Your Majesty, but I was told it's of grave importance."

"That it is." She announces to her court, "Everyone out, save you, Lord Henneth. Go on now."

Judging by the surprised looks from her fawning courtesans, I'd say her flatterers aren't used to being ousted. The men on either side of her remain put, but the rest of the court make their way out. With the audience chamber cleared and the door sealed, the queen continues.

"This is Lord Akkis Arnaut, Minister of Royal Affairs."

The pampered man bows his head. "Welcome to Her Majesty's court," he says with an embellished wave of his wrist.

"And this is First Marshall of my guard, Sir Hewett Gilliam."

Sir Gilliam says, "I believe your brother served in the guard back in King Darmin's day."

"Yes, he was a knight, Sir Anthus Whitefoot," I say. My brother had been much older than me, so I hardly knew him, but I knew he'd served the crown with honor. "He died in the Battle of Kiplinger when I was young."

"A famous battle at a critical juncture in our history. He died a valiant death. A sad loss for our kingdom."

The queen says, "These men are my closest advisers. I trust them with my life, as I do Lord Henneth, who summoned you here. Who is the young lady standing beside you?"

I introduce Sera, who seems to be holding up quite well under the queen's scrutiny. She's wearing the best outfit she owns, a coarse beige gown once her mother's, tied at the waist with a petaled flower blooming in red thread below her left shoulder and worn goatskin shoes that appear as if chewed on by the farmer's dog. Not that my weather-beaten garb is anything to croon about. "My apprentice, Sera of Saplinger, Your Majesty."

"You're awfully young, but I suppose that's to be expected of an apprentice. Welcome to my court, Sera of Saplinger."

Sera curtsies. "Thank you, Your Majesty."

The queen turns her attention to the matter at hand. "What I'm about to tell you doesn't leave this chamber, Ellis Whitefoot. Do you understand?"

I incline my head. "Yes, Your Majesty."

"By now, I assume you've heard rumors about the disappearance of arcanists from my kingdom."

"I've heard there's a shortage of available arcanists, Your Majesty, and a terrible rumor about the University closing, but nothing to speak of disappearances."

"Then I will fill you in. Someone has been dispatching my arcanists. And by dispatching, I mean killing them." Gods, it's far worse than I've heard. "At first we believed King Anders to be the culprit. He's been posturing against me for a decade. When I refused his hand in marriage, he declared my kingdom in violation of territory he claimed as belonging to the Kingdom of Althania, his so-called South Terran. His great-great-great-grandfather had conceded the land to us after losing the Battle of Auran Bay, and it's been called Northland ever since. King Devin Anders, who's earned the name Devin the Mad, and rightfully so, refuses to acknowledge it even after all this time. He's nothing like his father, unfortunately, so I've had to suffer his ambition and indignation, as well as rising tensions along our mutual border and ensuing clashes just short of all-out war. Nonetheless, Anders is a fool and a coward, not to mention his treasury is insolvent. His overtaxed territories are on the brink of rebellion thanks to his unrestrained extravagance. I don't believe Anders has the mind to assassinate my arcanists. However . . ."

The queen pauses to shift her bountiful proportions on her throne.

"It doesn't mean the Kingdom of Althania isn't culpable for this most heinous crime. My Chief Arcanist, Ruel, attended a parley on my behalf to try to smooth relations between kingdoms and to get to the root of the matter. He came back to us dead, burned to a crisp.”

I open my mouth, stunned. Ruel was a beloved arcanist, a man of immeasurable talent. To learn he's gone . . .

“My condolences, Your Majesty. Ruel was a bright light for our kingdom.”

“He was, and I mourn his loss each day. As for the University, I'm afraid the rumor you heard is true: it's closed until further notice. We lost prominent University professors, celebrated arcanists of great import. Mysterious deaths, all of them. I've lost some of the most brilliant minds in my kingdom. These are assassinations, Ellis Whitefoot. Don't believe otherwise.”

I can hardly stand the ill news. I feel it constrict around my chest and sour my stomach.

Sera's looking at me, perhaps wondering if I'm next. Dear child, if you only knew how laughable that is.

Lord Arnaut takes his turn speaking. His voice is as silky as the smooth skin of his plentiful jowls. “Her Majesty suspects our rival nation at work against us, but like her, I don't believe King Anders has it in him to devise such machinations. He's a dimwit and a loudmouth, as we all know. He could never orchestrate something as complex as an assassination in a foreign country while unable to control his domestic affairs. I would posit the killer is among us, waiting for the right moment to usurp the throne. A citizen of Warren, not Althania. And a slippery one at that to have eluded capture thus far.”

Sir Hewett lets out an exasperated breath. “Contrary to your assertion, Lord Arnaut, King Anders very much knows what he's doing. I would agree that his brilliance is lacking, but he's no fool. His extravagances might have gotten him in trouble, but he sees a way out—taking Warren by force. Someone is pulling his strings, the same someone responsible for the murder of our arcanists. Our spies tell us that a new power is rising to supplant the king. If the villain seizes the throne and is able to unite the squabbling territories behind him, then we will face a formidable threat. If that same villain possesses mastery over the arcane arts, it could spell doom for all of us."

Lord Arnaut huffs. "My dear Sir Hewett, were you at the parley in Althania? No, but I was. Not only was our very own beloved Chief Arcanist murdered in cold blood, but so was the Althanian Chief Arcanist. I saw his body with my own eyes. Some other devilry is at play, something that threatens both of our kingdoms."

I say the name of Althania's Chief Arcanist before I realize I'm speaking out of turn. "Mortimer Allagant is dead?"

Lord Arnaut lifts a painted eyebrow. "You knew the man?"

"I knew him briefly while I attended the University as a young man. We were classmates my first year. A long time ago." I would add that it was my only year, but the queen and her advisers don't need to know that. "He was clever, cunning, haughty, if not belligerent, but he was also a talented arcanist, perhaps the most talented among our kingdoms. No disrespect to Ruel, of course." I leave it at that, omitting the part about how Allagant took pleasure in my misfortune, making a laughingstock of me in front of my classmates, and ultimately convincing the faculty to expel me.

"Mortimer Allagant might be dead," Sir Hewett says, "but the assassination of the two Chief Arcanists happened in Althania. A magician of extraordinary power is behind this, perhaps now in control of the kingdom. Rest assured, he is planning our demise, using Anders' fear and paranoia against him to control him and do his bidding. Without the combined might of our arcanists, we are vulnerable to attack. The enemy knows this. Your Majesty, we should disallow the upcoming Althanian visit until we get our house in order. Otherwise, we could be inviting doom to our kingdom."

Lord Arnaut puffs up like a dressed suckling pig. "And I say the killer is here, hiding among us, plotting a coup. How else could you explain the loss of our beloved arcanists? The enemy is within our borders. Your Majesty, now more than ever, we need to ensure peace with Althania. Disallowing us the opportunity to strike a peace accord at this crucial time would be devastating. We have a common enemy, evidenced by the murder of both Chief Arcanists. It's prudent we allow the king to visit so we can forge an alliance to deal with this threat."

Sir Hewett stomps his boot. "This is ridiculous and downright dangerous. Your Majesty, we should forestall our meeting with the king. I implore you to call it off."

Lord Arnaut snorts even louder. "And I say Sir Hewett is the one being ridiculous, Your Majesty, for getting in the way of peace when war is knocking on our door!"

The queen cuts in. "Enough bickering!" Her shrill voice echoes hurtfully in my ears. "Yes, we are on the brink of war with that moose of a king. While I agree with you, Sir Hewett, that King

Anders would love nothing more than to annex Warren and refill his coffers, I must also agree with Lord Arnaut that if we disallow his scheduled visit, it could be a detriment to our peace. Going to war is not in our best interest. Many would suffer and die and nothing good could come of it. King Anders has agreed to another parley, this time monarch to monarch, and he's coming here—at my invitation, I remind you—and will be arriving two days hence in Isla Kay, where we will receive him. This gives us little opportunity to discover the malefactor behind the tragedies that have befallen us. I want answers, and I want them today. Ellis Whitefoot." My back goes rigid upon hearing my name. "How do we get to the bottom of this? How do we find our killer, whom Lord Arnaut asserts is hiding here, waiting for the right moment to take my throne from me?"

I'm ill equipped to give an answer, but this is the queen, and one doesn't snub the queen. "I suppose the first step is for someone to inquire at the Arcanist Guild, Your Majesty. Surely, someone knows something about what happened to the arcanists."

"You mean *you* should inquire, isn't that correct?"

Sera nods, encouraging me to give the only answer the queen wants to hear. "That's what I meant, Your Majesty."

"You would be wise to use discretion during your inquiry. Fortune favors the cautious in these uncertain times, especially one of magical abilities like yourself. Secrecy is a must, is it not?"

"Of course, Your Majesty. I shall avail myself to secrecy upon this urgent matter."

"Then it's settled. From this point forward, you will lead this investigation as my personal arcanist. Use whatever resources you need, but find the murderer. You will report directly to Lord Arnaut, as he is Minister of Royal Affairs, and this falls under his purview. He will direct anything vital to me. Lord Henneth will accompany you, both as protection and as an official representative in my name. Do you understand?"

But, but . . .

There are so many buts, I don't know where to begin.

"You look like you have a question. Do you, Arcanist Whitefoot?"

Yes, I do. My first question is: why me? My second is: can I get out of this obligation? My third is—

Sera shakes her head. She's a better adviser to me than I suspect either of the men standing beside the queen.

"No, Your Majesty."

The queen's rouged cheeks lift to accommodate a victorious smile. "Excellent. That'll be all." Then, with a squeak, she adds, "Don't disappoint me, Ellis Whitefoot. The kingdom depends on you."

* * *

LORD HENNETH AND two of his cavalrymen escort us on horseback to the Arcanist Guild, which sits betwixt the desirable neighborhood of Bingsbury and the destitute stinklot of Fender's Quarter, which the locals affectionately call Lousebottom. Our horses clip-clop over chipped cobbles, muted by the dense fog. The air carries the scent of seawater from the Narrows, mixed with wet stone.

"You do realize I have no idea what I'm doing."

Sera puffs her cheeks and mimics the queen's high-pitched voice. "You're not going to disappoint me, are you?"

"You mustn't joke like that!" I expect Lord Henneth and his men to wheel about and proclaim us as treasonous, but they continue on their unmerry way.

Sera stifles a giggle. "You should have seen the look on your face." Then she says, "But that was crass and I apologize."

"Apology accepted. As I was saying . . ."

"You have no idea what you're doing."

"Correct."

"Yet you are Ellis Whitefoot, Basilisk Slayer and the Savior of Saplinger."

That brings a smile to my face. "It's quite catchy, I must say. Your uncle would have a different opinion. It's not like I left your town . . . intact."

"Just imagine what might have happened if the basilisk had not been slain. It might have gone after the children. A few toppled timbers is a small price to pay."

"It was more than a few."

"Then we'll call it a draw."

"Agreed. That still doesn't help me figure out what we're going to do."

The rhythm of our horses' hooves falls in unison for a span of breath before resuming their discord. "What *are* we going to do?" Sera asks.

I was hoping one of the gods would come down to succor us

or bestow some miracle upon us. In lieu of that, I say, "We're going to the guild to get answers. Whoever's there will fill us in as to what's become of all the arcanists. Surely, one or more must be alive and well."

"The queen blames King Anders. Sir Hewett agrees, but Lord Arnaut says Mortimer Allagant is dead, so how could Althania be behind the murders? It's quite troubling."

"Yes, quite troubling indeed. To lose one Chief Arcanist is a tragedy. But to lose two . . . These men were icons. Their loss, along with the deaths of the other arcanists, is a terrible blow."

"How well did you know them?"

I grip my reins firmly, conjuring up old, painful memories. "Well enough to know their strengths and failings. Ruel was a rude, conceited lad when we were students at the University. The rudeness tempered with age, as it often does. He even extended a formal apology to me in his later years for his antics at school. A noble gesture, although the damage had already been inflicted, the wounds scarred over but never gone. Ruel was cocky and ambitious as a young man. He took pleasure in making me feel like a failure. But Mortimer—well, he was worse. You might say he was downright cruel. One time, he locked me in the Alchemy laboratory, but not before spilling a vial of toxic anthanis extract on the floor; I was sick for a week from the fumes. Then he swapped my wand in our Talisman workshop when I wasn't looking with one that was nearly identical, but completely inert. I spent three days trying to figure out what was wrong with it. My professor cited my ineptitude as 'calamitous and inexcusable' in front of our class, and I was rewarded with jeers from Mortimer and his cronies. There were other incidents just as malicious." I loosen my grip on the leather straps and flex my cramped fingers. "A word to the wise: if you're to survive the arcanum world, do try your best not to draw unnecessary attention to yourself. Take it from someone who knows better than most."

Sera lends me a sympathetic smile. "I'm sorry they were mean to you. They had no right."

"Oh, they had every right. They were virtuosos, loved by their professors and deified by their peers. I was, well, what would you call someone of my feeble abilities? A novice? An acolyte? A jester? They were only doing what was in their nature. Look what they'd become: revered arcanists, advisers to monarchs. There is no higher honor, my dear."

"But they're dead, and the queen's turned to you. I'd say there's honor in that, too."

May the gods bless this young lady for her kind and inexperienced heart. "Yes, there's that, I suppose. However, the loss of Ruel the Bold and Mortimer the Gray is catastrophic for both kingdoms. I mean, how could anyone best Ruel Bisset or Mortimer Allagant? It would require someone of extraordinary skill, no one I've ever heard of. A sorcerer of the dark arts, or perhaps a wizard in league with the god of night, or maybe . . ."

"Or maybe it's just someone with a black heart who's found the right opportunity."

I pause and peer at this young lass. She has the mind for the University, and much more. "Or someone like that."

We come to a stop in front of a gnarled wooden door with a plaque hanging over the entryway that depicts a curved branch from the Quellen tree and the motto, *Circuem Arcanum: Circle of Magic.*

"We've arrived." I present the disheveled building with the cracks in the crumbling stonework to my new apprentice. "Welcome to the Arcanist Guild of Ravenmore."

Inside, the cloying air reeks of mold and peat. An old woman with a hip that sways jerkily like a pendulum leads us to an office where a bushy-browed man of short stature sits minding a stinky pile of oiled sardines. He licks his fingers and comes to his feet.

"Amelda, how many times have I asked you to notify me when we have visitors?"

She scoffs. "And how many times is that, you old fool?" She looks at us and says, "He's all yours," and waddles off down another dim corridor.

The man, dressed in a waistcoat too large for his body, bows his head before Lord Henneth. "Ilven Gaisen at your service, milord. To whom do I owe this esteemed honor?"

Lord Henneth steps aside to allow Ilven to see me.

I smile politely. "Hello, Ilven."

"You?" His bushy eyebrows tent like vaulting caterpillars. Then he breaks into a fit of snorting laughter that has Henneth and his men exchanging questioning glances. I laugh, too, because this old geezer is none other than the Arcanum Entrustor, a fancy title for guild warden, the man responsible for its day-to-day operations. He's not an arcanist, but his job is no less important. "What brings you to Ravenmore? How long has it been, anyway?"

"Far too long," I say. "It's good to see you, old chap."

"Likewise. I never thought I'd see you again, especially after last time."

Ah, yes, last time.

The last time I'd been here was under unfortunate circumstances. It was right after I'd made a mess of Duke Arold's keep and word had reached the guild that a certain arcanist had made a dog's breakfast of our craft. I was—how should I put it?— unwelcome to return to the guild until I'd made amends with the duchy. Of course, that never happened. I wouldn't go as far as to say I was formally banned by the guild, but it might as well have been the case. "As did I. I'm here on the queen's business. This is Lord Henneth from the Queen's Guard, and his men. This is Sera, my apprentice."

Ilven's brows knit together when he sees Sera. "A pleasure to meet you, young lady."

"Likewise," she says.

I get to the meat of the matter. "Ilven, where is everyone? It can't just be you and Amelda, can it? This place is empty."

A shadow falls over Ilven's face. "Aye, empty now for over a month. First, Jamus disappeared without saying anything to anyone. Then he was found dead by the river, charred as if struck by lightning. Terrible, terrible! Old Kirkum was next. He was discovered in Lousebottom with his eyes put out. Sheela, poor gal, ended up in an alley, her dress blackened like tar. It was as if they'd picked a fight with a god and lost. It's so sad. They all worked at the University, as you well know. I could go on, but—" He shakes his head. I'm at a loss as to what to say. Despite having a contentious past with these arcanists, I still respected them. They were my brothers and sisters, even if they didn't profess to be, even if they thought of me as a second-rate arcanist, a bumbler of magic, an embarrassment to the profession.

"Surely there's been an investigation."

Ilven bobs his head. "There was. Ruel headed up the investigation himself, aided by Myra Lockhardt, the University's Inquisitor General. They believed Althania had sent over an assassin to kill our arcanists. They demanded counsel with Mortimer and the king to get to the bottom of this. Mortimer, in turn, insisted we were to blame for the deaths on his side. Ruel and Myra left for Althania. Ruel returned dead, Myra vanished inexplicably, and Mortimer was announced deceased by royal decree, apparently murdered, just like Ruel."

"Lord Arnaut said he saw the bodies with his own eyes."

"Then it's as I've feared. A great evil is at work. Black sorcery of the blackest kind. The night god is behind it, that treacherous witch. Mark my words!"

I feel my lips and cheeks pale at this disastrous news. Gods don't meddle in human affairs. But the night god . . .

"What about the others? Where's Orden? How about Keriline and Lews?"

Ilven rubs his weathered knuckles with a thumb. "Gone. All gone. The queen ordered the University shuttered after the fatalities mounted. The few arcanists that were left standing scattered to the winds. And why wouldn't they, when their kind has been decimated? I'm no arcanist, so I suppose I've been spared. But you, Ellis, are you not afraid for your own life?"

If I wasn't before, I am now. Sera's eyes are wide with fear, poor thing. I imagine she's never had to deal with murder, not in her small town. I certainly haven't, not in all of my years or all of my travels.

This is bad.

Bad, bad, bad.

I refuse to answer his question, but instead ask my own. "Is there no one left?"

He stares off, troubled, rubbing his knuckles in earnest. He doesn't want to tell me, but I can wait until the candle on his table burns out if I must. At last, he looks at me and says, "I'm sorry, dear Ellis, but you're all that's left."

* * *

"I CANNOT ALLOW THIS," Lord Henneth says to me. "The queen gave me strict orders."

I tell him, "And the queen gave me orders to find the killer."

"You want to go to Lousebottom? By yourselves? No, I will not permit it. Your safety is my responsibility."

"I thank you for that, Lord Henneth, truly I do, but if he sees a royal escort, he'll scare away. Sera and I must go alone."

"I won't allow it."

"Fine. Then let's go to the queen and tell her we've failed. Let's see how that goes."

The obdurate lord ponders my sharp response, wiggling his

iron jaw. Then he says, "Very well, but if you come back emptyhanded, that's on you."

Duly noted, my thickheaded friend.

I bow graciously. "Your generosity is greatly appreciated, milord."

With that, Sera and I take what's left of the afternoon and head on our way.

Lousebottom isn't for the weak-hearted, mind you. It's where the fleas dance on the backs of sickly dogs and cutthroats live in the shadows among the poor. The lovely odors that waft in the heavy air remind me that rolling in mud is a privilege compared to coming here. Sera pinches her nose.

"How can you stand the smell?"

"Sheer will," I say. It's the truth. Even the basilisk's lair smelled better than this shanty of dilapidated dwellings. Most of the shutters are either closed or hanging at odd angles, as if winking at us.

"What makes you think he still lives here?"

"Because he's Borgess Copperton. He's an odd one, you'll see, a consummate creature of habit. Like I said, he knows everyone at the University. He's worked at the library for almost forty years."

"Yet he lives in Lousebottom."

"Did I mention he's odd? By the way, don't stare at his eyes. He's a bit, let's just say, cockeyed."

We tie off our horses outside a house tilted to one side as if a single breath might take it down. I pray our steeds are still there when we return. The floorboards creak underfoot as I step up to knock.

The man who greets us at the door has a wild beard as long as his skinny forearm, twice as long as I remember, with nary a hair up top, which isn't unexpected, seeing as he was balding at a young age. But it's his infectious smile that hasn't changed, big and bright, lighting up the dim and damp interior of a home that's been in his family since his great-grandfather's era. It smells like a wet forest in here, the wood slats on the walls matching with their mossy green color.

"Heronium Ellis Whitefoot! Gods be good, you're alive, you crooked mage!" He embraces me as if I'm his long-lost brother, and I have to admit, I've missed him too. I give him a strong pat on the back.

"It's good to see you, you old coot."

I introduce Sera, whom he takes an immediate liking to. "First, young lady, I bid you a sincere welcome to my auspicious dwelling. Second, I must ask: how did you get mixed up with the likes of this masquerader of magic? And an apprentice, no less. Has he taught you anything yet?"

Sera, sweet and kind Sera, says, "He's planning on teaching me a great many things. Once we've completed the queen's business, that is."

One of Borgess' eyes is on me, the other on Sera. "The queen's business? Do tell. Better yet, let me put on a pot of tea."

With cups filled to the brim and gathered around a wobbly table before the hearth, I proceed to explain my conscription into the queen's service and the task at hand. Herbaceous, steaming tea masks the moldy air.

"My apologies to the both of you," Borgess says. "Especially you, Sera. You probably thought you'd be living a life of grandeur being the apprentice to an arcanist. You poor, misguided thing. How's the tea?"

Sera smiles politely. She's taken one sip. "Hot."

"An accurate answer, but also an objectively neutral one. Ellis, this one is made for the queen's court."

The tea is bitter, almost undrinkable. "What is this stuff?"

"I helped myself to a jar of Lillian root before they shuttered the University. It's a soothing decoction for these troubling times. Drink up. It's not poison, I assure you. Well, not in small doses."

I steer us to the looming topic. "Ilven shared the dire news of what happened to Jamus, Kirkum and Sheela. Then there's Ruel and Mortimer, among others."

"Mortimer too? No, I hadn't heard that."

"It's true. A grievous loss for our community. Ilven believes there's black sorcery involved. He thinks there's a magician who's in league with the night god. Preposterous? I don't know. The question remains: who could have done this?"

"Who indeed?" Borgess blows ripples across the surface of his tea, then takes a hearty swallow. "Ilven is superstitious, but I can't fault him. There are ten gods, but the night god is feared above all, a meddler in mortal affairs, the legends say. They call her Shevra. The Shade Queen. Mistress of Death. And many other names. The necromancers of yore revered her, prayed to her, and supposedly they had made a pact with her to give up their lives and become her undying servants in exchange for channeling her power to serve their ugly deeds. But that was a century ago. The question we should ask ourselves is: why? Why kill the most talented minds of our generation?"

"The obvious answer is elimination of competition and consolidation of power. Sir Hewett Gilliam believes Althania is behind this and their king has fallen under the spell of a puppeteer who is using him to get to Warren. Lord Arnaut disagrees, citing Mortimer's death as proof that both kingdoms are in peril, and that the killer is here in Ravenmore, biding his time for an opportune strike against the throne. Maybe that time is when King Anders arrives in Isla Kay in two days' time to parley with the queen."

Borgess gives the cracked rim of his cup a thoughtful rub of his thumb. "What if Gilliam and Arnaut are both right? What if the king is a puppet and the puppeteer's agent is operating here in Ravenmore, waiting patiently for this meeting to happen? It would be the perfect opportunity to kill both monarchs and seize power. With both monarchs deposed, a single kingdom will arise under this usurper and his agent, and no arcanists will be around, able to stop them. Well, there's you, of course. Cheers to that." He toasts the air and drinks.

I manage an uneasy smile. Sera comes to my aid. "You shouldn't underestimate Ellis. He saved my town. I've witnessed the result of his skills and quick thinking firsthand."

Borgess wipes his lips with the back of his hand. "No offense to my dear friend, but I've witnessed it too. But I'm sure his results were flawless in your town's case." Borgess doesn't mean to jab at me, but he's, well, Borgess.

Sera looks at me, worried I might be upset if she reveals the truth about what I did to Saplinger. Alas, the truth has followed me all of my life. Not often has it helped my cause.

"If we can get back to the matter, please." I'm stern but well-mannered, as one should be as a guest of the ever-eccentric Borgess Copperton. "If there is an assassin in Ravenmore waiting for the king of Althania to arrive, how do I find him? Or her? Surely there's a traitor among our kind, someone lured to the dark arts, perhaps a disgruntled professor or student, or maybe a necromancer or disciple of the night god."

"Did Ilven tell you how Jamus and the others were killed?"

"He indicated an arcane origin. Charred by lightning, black as tar, eyes put out, I believe were his descriptions."

"Yes, burned perhaps, but fire can do that as well, can it not?"

"What are you suggesting?"

Borgess presses his lips into a swirl of a smirk. "Before Ruel headed off to Althania, he and the Inquisitor General had assumed the same—that the deaths of the arcanists were caused by magic— yet they documented an anomaly, which, by law, found its way into the Scroll of Record, a copy of which was required to be shelved in the Archives, my domain. That anomaly, which I overlooked originally, has bothered me since. It speaks of the victims' blood, what little there was, being 'the color of smoke.' I had thought, 'Borgess, this is not the work of fire.' Besides, not all of the victims had died a cindery death. No, there was something else at work. As a failed potionist, my love of herbs and tinctures has never left me.

The blackened blood was clearly the effect of a toxin, not magic nor fire. It was from a tincture, an insidious drop of a special extract. You might recall such an extract in one of your misadventures."

At this point, I think Borgess is deliriously mad, his imagination getting the better of him. But that swirl on his lips, that luminous smirk, it's undeniable. "Anthanis extract? Like the one Mortimer used to make me sick?"

"One and the same, yes. But don't blame dear old Mortimer. It's not as uncommon as you think. In a tea, like this for example, it would be impossible to discover the villain until after you've gone to sleep and never woke up again. Anthanis extract was made to be a sleep elixir, but, in a high-enough dose, it's lethal."

I can still taste the fumes, that pine needle oil on my tongue, that noxious burn in my nostrils from the extract. Allagant had spilled it on the floor. But if I had ingested it . . .

"So, they were poisoned?" The revelation is unexpected, considering how Ilven described the dead arcanists. He thought them killed by magic. How could he have known otherwise?

"I'm afraid so," Borgess says. "I can't fathom any other conclusion."

"I must inform Lord Arnaut at once." I'm ready to leave, to head back, but Borgess stops me with his long, skinny fingers.

"A word of caution," he says. "Trust no one, dear Ellis. If you learned anything at the University, it should be that."

* * *

MY MIND IS REELING from Borgess' revelation.

Could the arcanists have been poisoned?

Would it be so far-flung that the bodies were doctored after the fact, made to look like a master arcanist assassin had done them in?

Which makes me wonder what happened to Ruel and my old nemesis, Allagant, whose antic with the extract had become a deadly end for a respected group of arcanists.

Sera is thinking about it too as Lord Henneth and his cavalrymen lead us back to the citadel. In a low voice she says, "You should speak to the queen about this. It's too important to go through Arnaut. I don't trust him."

Sera has good instincts for her age, strong opinions, too, but in this case, our hands are tied. In a voice as quiet as hers, and out of earshot of our escort, I say, "The queen was clear about how information is to be communicated. Lord Arnaut first, then if he deems the information of value, he'll pass it along to her. I don't see how I can circumvent his authority. Do you?"

Sera doesn't, and so we are forced to present ourselves to the perfume-scented Lord Arnaut.

"You were wise to bring this information directly to me." Lord Arnaut is wearing a silk toga doused in heady flower oils. He looks like a swine lavishly clad in finery. "I will be sure to let Her Majesty know." He graces us with a supercilious smile. It's his way of letting us know he has no intention of telling the queen.

"I think it would be prudent for us to present the information to the queen together, milord, given the severity."

"I said I would inform her. Or did I not make myself clear?"

"Yes, but—"

"That'll be all, Arcanist Whitefoot. Prepare yourself for our journey on the morrow. We leave for Isla Kay at first light. And by 'prepare,' I mean bathe. You stink like a sewer. The same goes for your pet. Good day."

Sera is about to say something detrimental to our wellbeing, I can tell, so I firmly stop her with a widening of the eyes. She relents, thank goodness.

At least the queen's perfumed hog is kind enough to allow us to clean up at the royal bathhouse. A dip in the hot mineral springs, fresh clothing, and Sera and I are civilized once more, although Sera is still brooding over our encounter with Lord Arnaut. We're given an apartment in the palace with a balcony facing the Narrows and the harbor below. Tomorrow, we depart for the seaport of Isla Kay, a briny refuge at the very tip of the isthmus that marks the northernmost edge of the kingdom. I smell a delicious aroma and follow my nose to a plentiful tray of bread, fruits and cheeses sitting by the open window. I slather butter onto a thick slice of bread while Sera sulks.

"Aren't you hungry? I'm famished." It's evening now, cool and clear, with a splash of peach against the dimming sky.

"I don't feel like eating." Sera folds her arms.

"Come now, you have to eat. This is a veritable feast."

"Can you believe the gall of that man? He dismissed us like we were serfs."

I nibble on a bit of cheese with a rich aroma and a hint of an herb I can't quite place as I spread a princely portion of dripping honeycomb atop my bread. "Yes, and then he thought he'd mollycoddle us with a hot bath and scented oils, as if we were part of the royal furniture. It's insulting, I know, but you mustn't allow it to eat away at you. This is the way of court life, I'm afraid."

"Is it? And we're expected to hope His High and Mighty reports our findings to the queen? It's rubbish."

I sink my teeth into the bread. My tongue levitates to the heavens. I doubt I will ever be able to relive this moment again, but I must address Sera's scowl, so I chew quickly. "I know what'll cheer you up."

She eyes me curiously. "What?"

"Remember when you asked to be my apprentice?"

"I believe that was your idea."

"Yes, yes, but back in the forest, while on our way to the basilisk's lair, I could see it in your eyes. Then you confessed your desire to come to Ravenmore to learn the craft, and well, I presented you to Lord Henneth as my apprentice. And to the queen. And everyone else."

"Your point?"

"My point is that I've been remiss. You've been an apprentice only in title, but you haven't learned anything of the craft."

A smile stretches across her face. "You're going to teach me the arcane arts?"

I hold out my hand. "Now, now, I didn't say that."

"But you said—"

"Yes, I said you should learn the craft. Learning the craft requires patience, student and teacher both. As such, I've never had an apprentice. In fact, I don't know the first thing about apprenticeship." Her smile droops, but I'm quick to add, "That said, I suppose I've been waiting my entire career for someone to come along to carry on what I've learned. Mind you, I'm not—how might I put it—*proficient* in my craft. If I am to be completely honest, I'm the worst example of an arcanist for anyone to follow. However"—I hold up a finger—"I know the foundation, the theory, and the mechanics. I might not express it so eloquently through my magical abilities, but in my mind, I'm the world's best arcanist."

Sera, unable to restrain herself, says, "And perhaps the only one."

"Yes, thank you for that lovely fact." I take a deep breath. The sea smells particularly wonderful this evening. "I would like to give you your first instruction as an apprentice."

"Really?" She claps like a giddy lass, but I can't but feel a bit of it myself.

"Yes, but under one condition: we eat. I can't teach you anything if I'm salivating like a wolf."

Sera laughs. "Very well, sir wolf, let us dine like nobles."

After our meal, I take out my wand. It's little more than the length of a stretched hand, three sections jointed in two places, like an aged finger. I've had this wand for four decades. The Quellen wood is dark, deep brown, and nearly unbreakable.

"Your Isabella," Sera says in admiration.

"Yes, she is." I smile fondly. "You should note the wand is the tool of an arcanist, an extension of the body, if you will. Never point it at another person unless you intend to use it. If you remember anything, remember that. Now, an arcanist holds a wand as such." I hold it delicately in my right hand, the bottom third gently grasped between my forefinger, thumb and middle finger. "You move it as if you imagine yourself dancing to a jig, like so." I wave the wand around, humming a tune, stressing my movements with the stresses in the tune. "Of course, we don't wield it with frenetic energy. We only move the wand to match our incantation. Here, you try."

As soon as Sera takes possession of the wand, I can tell she's a natural, a born arcanist. Her grip is delicate but assured, the flick of her wrist measured and graceful, the beat of each movement like the rise and fall of a musical scale. "Am I doing it right?"

I want to cry happy tears, the sight is so moving. "Quite well, yes. Now let's try an incantation."

I retrieve the wand and point at the single remaining wedge of cheese on our tray. "We're going to practice nudging the cheese along the platter. To do so, you're going to move the wand as so and repeat the following: *Illium Dimenstrum.*" In slow motion, I show the movement, then I stop and repeat the phrase, careful not to execute the incantation, as the two must be done in concert. "Now you try."

She does, but her flick is too strong, her phrase a breath too slow.

She tries again, but her timing is too quick. A third time causes the cheese to wiggle. A fourth nudges it a fraction. A fifth misses. She sighs, disappointed.

"You were close. Why did you stop?"

Sera looks at the wand, brushes the length with a fingertip. "I don't know. I had it, then I lost it. Show me how it's done." She hands the wand to me.

The evening sky is a lovely deep indigo now. I count to three, then recite the incantation while flicking my wrist as I showed her. The cheese not only moves, but the platter as well. Before I can contain the movement, the platter is flying out the open window, plunging to the rocks below, where I imagine it will strike in a dramatic fashion, before getting swallowed by the current.

I quickly hide my embarrassment, hoping the deepening red in my cheeks is masked by the poor daylight. "I meant to do that."

"You certainly nudged the cheese."

"Yes, well, there are many interpretations to the word 'nudge.'"

Sera grants me a merciful smile. "Shall we turn in for the night?"

Smart girl, she knows how to curtsey her way out of my disastrous first lesson. "Yes, let's."

* * *

DAWN BRINGS THE FOG, and with it a busy day. By midmorning, we're aboard a galley, headed through the channel into open water, where we will hug the coastline until evening. The queen's standard flaps strongly in the wind. Her Majesty is belowdecks while Lord Arnaut stands upon the bow with two more pampered types. Sir Gilliam is on the foredeck, clad in light armor beside a trio of knights. I imagine they're conversing on knightly affairs, including the finer tactics of defending a queen against a raving-mad king beguiled by a mastermind of magic.

With Sera by my side and several deckhands attending to their duties, I fix my gaze on Lord Arnaut, who's enjoying himself immensely as he holds court with his obsequious friends. Had he spoken to the queen about the poison? Did she believe him? Did she even care? Would our questions ever be answered or would they be ignored?

The stars peek out from a cloud-streaked sky as we dock at Isla Kay, little more than a stone fortification set upon a triangular bluff facing an endless horizon of ocean. The locals are a rough lot, appearing carved like the gray, windswept stone that encompasses the small promontory. We enter the keep and dine quietly in the grand hall as guests of Baron Rathford, who's had Isla Kay in his family for six generations. He's the queen's man for sure, muttonchops and gleaming blue eyes dancing to her every quip. By the time supper's over, we've had our fill of smoked fish, charred greens, roast potatoes and sour wine. The merriment commences with the lively dance of a fiddle. Sera's taken by the excitement and the newness, practicing wrists flicks in alignment with the song's fast tempo. I'm proud of her. I wish we could be done with this affair so I could teach her, really teach her what I know. With a disappointing first lesson, I vow to complete the next one without err.

I manage to catch Lord Arnaut at a moment when he's alone. He's been at the queen's side throughout dinner while Sir Gilliam's gone off to prepare for the arrival of the royal Althanian party, set to dock at daybreak. I drain the balance of my terrible wine and flag the lord down with my empty cup.

"Lord Arnaut, if I might have a word."

He lets out a bored breath. "What is it, Arcanist Whitefoot?"

I bite my tongue and reply pleasantly. "I'm anxious to find out what the queen had to say about the poison."

He hushes me, then drags me aside with his manicured fingers, which are much stronger than I imagined from a soft man like him. "You must be discreet, Arcanist Whitefoot, or have you forgotten the queen's order?"

I'm not used to being grabbed so, and my response reflects my ungentle reaction. "My order was to report my findings and for those findings to make it to the queen's ear, Lord Arnaut. The fact that the arcanists were poisoned to death and then made to look as if they were burned or destroyed by magic tells us the assassin isn't an arcanist, but rather an ordinary man, perhaps someone they trusted, someone known to them."

Lord Arnaut's rebuttal is swift and just as sharp. "Your proof comes from a man charged with looking after the library, a resident of Lousebottom no less. A man with anecdotal evidence, claiming his fact is written into the official record when it is not. A man whose opinion is opposite the Arcanum Entrustor's of the Arcanist Guild of Ravenmore, a trusted and respected custodian of this revered institution. Your man is no longer employed by the University due to his decaying sense of restraint. Or did your friend fail to tell you that?"

For a moment, everything is thrown into doubt. I know Borgess Copperton. He might be peculiar by most standards, perhaps no longer employed, assuming that's true, but he's no liar.

"Still," I say in the calmest and most respectful voice possible, "Her Majesty should be given the information, anecdotal or not, so that she might decide what's best for her kingdom. Did you do that?"

Lord Arnaut, pampered swine that he is, simply says, "It's none of your concern," and departs, leaving a scented trail of flower petals in his wake.

Sera, of course, is anxious to find out the result of my meeting. "How did it go?"

I put on an exaggerated smile. "Brilliantly."

"That well, huh?"

I look at my empty cup. Surely another fill of wretched wine couldn't hurt. "And I imagine tomorrow will go even better."

* * *

IT'S THE HANGOVER of the ages, but there's no room for feeling sorry for myself or adjusting slowly to the waking world.

Sera shakes me to consciousness. Sir Gilliam is standing in our room, outfitted in gleaming, oiled armor, embellished with tasteful scrollwork. What's he doing here?

"Her Majesty requires your immediate presence," he says. "Do try to rinse your mouth. You smell like the bottom of a fouled wine barrel."

Her Majesty is just as unhappy at my tardy appearance as Sir Gilliam was upon seeing me rise from bed. Sera's beside me, poor lass, trapped by the fact I've made her my unfortunate apprentice. I'm sorry, young lady, but you'll have to bear with me as I embarrass us into the cellars, where we will be left to dine with the rats until our untimely deaths.

I'm not prepared to see the queen waiting at a long table filled with nobles and statesmen, half of which are clearly not from our kingdom. We're in a meeting room high up in the keep with large, open windows offering a spectacular view of the sea and the surf crashing against the rocks below. My stomach falls out of my body when I realize that the queen is at one end, regally befitted in her cape and crown, opposite a gangly man in his thirties at the other end, outfitted in gaudy red silk over leather and a jeweled diadem over his high forehead. It doesn't take a magician to presume this is the one-and-only King Anders of Althania. How could I have overslept?

I bow before the queen and take my place at a seat beside a perky and irritated Lord Arnaut, whose demonic gaze is nothing short of terrifying. He would make quite the basilisk, given the opportunity.

"King Anders, forgive the late intrusion," Arnaut says on the queen's behalf. "This is Ellis Whitefoot, newly appointed to Her Majesty's council as guest arcanist until we can find a worthy replacement for our former Chief Arcanist. His evaluation of time seems to be out of proportion with the rest of Warren. Or Althania for that matter."

The queen is equally unhappy at my arrival, evidenced by her daggered gaze.

Clearly, I was set up. Or was it the wine?

Still, I can't help but think the perfumed menace is to blame.

Apparently, I stepped out of line last night with Lord Arnaut, fueled by an urgent sense of duty to the crown. Now, I've lost face with the queen.

I slink into the empty seat. Sera has the wisdom to hover along the back wall like a fly.

The queen says, "As I said before we were rudely interrupted, we must come to a consensus on this imminent threat. My kingdom is not the only one at stake. Yours is in peril, too, Devin."

King Anders seems unconcerned, angled back in his chair as if he'd already laid claim to Isla Kay on his conquest of the southernly kingdom of Warren. A woman, a comely adviser, whispers into his ear and he smiles. Behind them is a wall of intimidating knights in black-burnished armor.

"Esmerelda, I've journeyed here on good faith so we could come to an appropriate set of terms. You've given me a formal discourse on the mutual threat facing our kingdoms, and I appreciate your desire to work together. But it seems our respective appraisements of this threat differ from one another. You've lost a great many of your most respected arcanists, including Ruel the Bold, who died while visiting my city. I've suffered losses as well, but my losses are different than yours. I've lost South Terran, for example, which you call Northland, a territory that includes this very place where we sit."

The queen's rouged cheeks flash hot. "Seriously, Devin, you came all this way to bring that up again? How many times do I need to tell you, your forefather conceded the land to us? It is legally ours. Read your history texts."

"That's your made-up history, not ours. The land was taken from us. In fact, if you look at your own history books, you'll see that Warren is an Althanian territory, a territory that had been part of my family for a millennium when a traitorous ancestor of yours came along and took it from us. It wasn't conceded, as you claim."

The queen's shrill voice rises above the tumult of crashing waves. "Is this why you've come here, to lay claim to lost territories? We have dead mages, Devin. Or did you forget that your very own Chief Arcanist was felled by an assassin?"

King Anders leans forward, appetite growing in his eyes. No wonder he's earned the moniker, Devin the Mad. "And by whose account was my Chief Arcanist felled?"

The queen, utterly flustered, squeaks her response. "You know who, Devin. Don't play dumb."

Anders, clearly reveling in the queen's frustration, smiles for everyone to see. "Oh, you mean Lord Arnaut. The very man seated next to you. Your most trusted adviser, your Minister of Royal Affairs, who also happens to be the only witness to have seen my Chief Arcanist dead. I believe his written account stated that Mortimer Allagant was 'charred beyond recognition, as if the gods had come down and burned him with holy fire.' Lord Arnaut, would you say this is an accurate recitation?"

The queen looks at Lord Arnaut, as we all do, and I'm hit with the queasy sensation in the pit of my stomach that the sole witness to Mortimer Allagant's demise is the linchpin in our impending undoing.

Lord Arnaut rises from his seat, calmly and purposefully, not at all alarmed at the grave error he's being accused of. He's not as soft as he was a moment before, not as smooth-skinned or heavy around the waist. It's as if he's slimming before our eyes, growing a little more worn, a little more—what is the word I'm seeking?—*weathered.* Yes, weathered, both in age and appearance. I see it in Sera's eyes, too, and the queen's, even Sir Gilliam's, whose calm exterior seems suddenly shaken.

Lord Arnaut addresses the queen. "I wish to make a formal apology, Your Majesty." Even his voice has lost its unctuous smoothness, becoming more masculine, deeper and stronger. He moves behind me, working slowly down the long table along the sea-facing wall toward an anxiously awaiting Anders, who undoubtedly is eager to hear what the Minister of Royal Affairs has to say.

Arnaut pauses momentarily behind my left shoulder. I can feel the heat of his breath upon my back, sending chills up my neck.

The queen, resolute and bitter answers his request. "Let's hear it, Lord Arnaut."

"First, I would like to apologize for the delay in accurate reporting. Trust me, Your Majesty, I've waited with bated breath to speak the truth. Second, I'd like to apologize for the untimely death of Ruel Bisset, our dear, dear Ruel the Bold. He was the best of all of us, and he will be missed for as long as we remember his name."

Lord Arnaut gives my shoulder a strong squeeze, and he moves on to the next person, one of the queen's stunned nobles, another pampered pet. Arnaut's expanded gut is slimmed now and his toga clings loosely to his body. It's shorter as well, or maybe he's grown taller. I can't understand what I'm seeing.

"Third, I'd like to apologize to the House of Arnaut, whose namesake I bear. Lord Akkis Arnaut was a just man. Forgive him for his service to Warren. It shouldn't be marred for what he's done."

The queen speaks up. "Forgive him? What are you talking about, Akkis? And what is wrong with your . . . your stature? Or do my eyes deceive me in this light?"

"No, Your Majesty, your eyes don't deceive you. They are seeing what they should be seeing."

Arnaut continues to the next seat, this one occupied by a noble from House Anders, a thick man with a moustache that extends cheek to cheek and curls at the tips.

"My fourth and final apology, Your Majesty, is for the misreporting of the death of Mortimer Allagant, Mortimer the Gray as he was formally known. Mortimer the Redeemer as his name shall be set in the record books. Mortimer didn't die at the hand of an assassin. His body was never found, never witnessed by the king, as reported, nor by anyone else."

The queen, trembling with rage, pounds a fist on the table. I feel it too, punching a hole in my gut. "Are you bloody telling me you made this up? Are you telling me that Mortimer isn't dead? What about Ruel? Is he alive and well, too? What about Myra? Have they all formed an alliance, working together, conspiring and plotting against my kingdoms?" She's winded, as am I, both of us unable to keep our breathing in check.

"No, Your Majesty, that is not the case." Lord Arnaut works

his way over to the king while Queen Esmerelda fumes and all of us prepare to hear our fates handed to us. "The truth is Ruel the Bold is dead. Myra Lockhardt is dead, too. Many more arcanists are dead. These are facts. But Mortimer Allagant, Mortimer the Redeemer, isn't dead."

Arnaut, or what used to be Arnaut is behind the king now, hands firmly on his shoulders. Anders is smiling like a madman. I'm watching as Arnaut ages incredulously before my eyes, becoming thinner and older, his hair turning to gray.

My gods, it can't be!

"Mortimer Allagant is very much alive, Your Majesty," what used to be Arnaut says. "In fact, my dear Esmerelda, you are looking at him right now."

* * *

THE ROOM IS SILENT as a deserted dungeon, save for the unending pounding of the sea, much like the pounding of my heart.

The transformation is complete. Lord Arnaut is Mortimer Allagant!

How could I have not seen it? Or the queen? Or anyone else?

Not only has he infiltrated the highest ranks of Her Majesty's nobility, but he's brought the enemy to our gates.

All this time, we've thought the murderer was someone else. No one suspected Arnaut. And certainly not Allagant. Even after learning about the poisoning of the arcanists from Borgess, the same extract Mortimer Allagant had used on me all those years ago, I'd not thought Allagant was alive, nor the perpetrator.

How could I be such a fool?

Lord Gilliam is first to speak. "Your Majesty, let me arrest him right now."

As if spurred by his voice, all six knights of the Queen's Guard grip the pommels of their sheathed swords. The knights in black armor surrounding King Anders show no alarm, nor movement. And why should they? They have the most powerful arcanist in the land, perhaps the most powerful arcanist to ever live. I snake my hand slowly beneath the tabletop toward the inside of my vest where my wand hangs. If I can get to it, I might be able to do something.

And do what, Ellis, bring down another tower? Destroy another town? Toss a tray of cheese out the window?

My hand freezes.

I'm a coward. I've always been a coward.

The queen stands, bristling among her knights. "How dare you! How dare you gain my trust and deceive me? Devin, was this part of your plan all along? To come here and demand I relinquish your precious South Terran, because it once belonged to your ancestors? Or have you come here to demand I turn over my entire kingdom? Because you can dismiss that notion right now."

Allagant pats King Anders on the shoulder, relieving him of any speaking responsibility. The king relaxes in his seat like a good dog. The true master has arrived.

"His Majesty was content living an exorbitant life, unlike his father, who ruled to serve his people. I can't blame Devin for his wants or desires. Sure, he'd love to get back South Terran, but only for the sake of besting you, Your Majesty, because you turned his hand down in marriage."

"This is because of that?"

"No, not in the least," Allagant says. "This is about a new era, one that I've been planning for some time. You see, the king is deep in debt. He's overleveraged and overextended his rule, and the country's reserves are now barren, with additional monies owed to a host of lords and ladies he's borrowed from. If not for me, they would have stormed his castle and dragged him from his bed into the streets for a public execution. But I'm resourceful. Vast riches lay to the south, here in Warren. I've laid out a plan for the nobility of Althania. Stay the course while I neutralize the opposition and I will unite north and south into a single kingdom. For that, the king will be spared his life, his financial obligations repaid, and a new ruler shall take the scepter to govern a kingdom that hasn't been one land for over a thousand years. Do you know what they said, Your Majesty? Do you have any idea? They said yes. Unequivocally yes. And here I am to fulfill that promise."

The queen's trembling has reached the uncontrolled stage now. I fear not for my life, but Sera's. She shouldn't be here, yet she is stuck in this room. The queen's shrill voice curdles my ears. "How dare you, Mortimer Allagant! You have no noble blood. You're nothing but a servant and a murderer and a turncoat. High treason demands death, and you must face it!"

Allagant, unmoved by the threat, answers in kind. "I am giving you until the morrow to remove yourself from office. Renounce your throne and proclaim me as ruler of New Althania, and I will spare your life and the lives of your nobles. By doing so, you will avoid bloodshed. You will save those who serve you. Defy me and you will pay the ultimate price for your defiance."

"You might be a powerful wizard, but this stronghold is filled with soldiers who will lay down their lives to defend the crown. Don't take my word for it. Ask Lord Gilliam or any of the others. Come now, you know us well enough."

Again, Allagant is calm. He smiles at me. "Hello, Ellis, enjoying the show? Not going for your wand, are you?"

My hand is stuck where it is, frozen in a cowardly position.

"That's what I thought. Your Majesty, to address your concern over my safety, I would like to turn your attention out to sea. Cast your eyes upon the waters. Search the horizon. What do you see?"

Lord Gilliam is the first to spot them. "Warships! Those are warships, Your Majesty."

The room erupts into commotion. I'm compelled to look. Across the hazy distance, I pick out shapes on the water. Dozens of ships. An entire fleet.

"Not just warships," Allagant says, speaking in an unhurried but authoritative tone. "I have an army at my back as well. Well-armed, well-supplied cavalry and foot soldiers, eager to reclaim their ancestors' land. The time for surrender has come. Both my ships and my army will reach this shore just before dawn. You might try to mount your defenses and sack my fleet from here, but my army will overtake this stronghold with ease. Isla Kay was never meant to be more than a forward fortification, a signaling point to give early warning to Ravenmore so that it might defend the

Narrows against invaders. I'll admit it, taking Ravenmore would be nigh impossible without mass casualties. But if I enter unimpeded, with the queen a vassal of New Althania, no bloodshed will be required. Your people will continue to live in peace, the same as now, but with new landlords, new taxes, and a new sense of direction for a kingdom that will run sea to sea. I will give you your own territory to occupy until old age, wife to the former King Anders, now my newly appointed Regent of New Althania. What do you say, Queen Esmerelda? Relinquish Warren. Allow peace to run its course."

The queen is so mad she can hardly speak, but she does, and the shrillness in her voice is diminished to a fiery rasp. "I shall not concede under any condition, you traitorous murderer!"

Sir Gilliam draws his sword as do the other knights. Allagant's knights hold fast as their master withdraws his wand. The tip glows red like a setting sun.

"Might I suggest, Your Majesty, that you have your men stand down? There's no need to spill blood. And trust me, mine will not be the blood that's spilled."

The queen's face is almost as red as the tip of Allagant's wand. She turns to me. "Are you just going to sit there, mage? You're my arcanist, are you not? Defend your queen! Defend your kingdom!"

All eyes fall on me and I can feel my cheeks grow hot.

There's something I have to do, but I don't quite know how to do it.

Allagant makes the decision for me. "Ellis, dear chap, do us both a favor and stay your hand. You don't need to take one last catastrophe to the grave."

I slowly withdraw my hand, as if someone else is doing it. I can't look up. I can't face the queen. I certainly can't face Sera.

I've failed.

Mortimer Allagant levels one more insult before striding with his soldiers and former king across the room. "That's exactly how I remember you, Ellis, and it's exactly how you shall be remembered."

To the queen he says, "You have until morning. Lay down your weapons and surrender, or lay down your lives."

* * *

"IT'S NOT YOUR FAULT," Sera tells me.

"Really? Are we not in the cellar, listening to the waves smash against the rocks as the salt soaks into our skin and the stink of the sea fills our nostrils?"

"He let you keep your wand."

How kind of him. After we were excused, Allagant relayed orders that Sera and I were to enjoy some quiet time in the cellar of the keep, detained in a cave-like storage space that doubles as a dungeon. I imagine the queen didn't object, especially after my poor showing during our doomed parley.

Not only have I failed my queen, but I've failed all of Warren.

I've failed my apprentice, too. Sera is kind, but I know she expected more of me. She expected me to act, to stand up to Mortimer Allagant, to be the same arcanist who risked his life against a basilisk. What am I now?

A disappointment.

It seems that will be my legacy. Ellis the Disappointer.

Or Ellis the Coward, the arcanist who allowed his kingdom to get taken by a criminal, a despot and a murderer.

Or Ellis Whitefoot, the arcanist who lived up to his curse.

Is that who I am?

Is that all I am?

No, it's not. That's not how I want to be remembered.

That's not how I want Sera to remember me.

"There is one way to save us," I say as strongly as the salt-soaked words coming from my mouth. "I face Mortimer Allagant one-on-one, as allowed under the arcanist law of Trial by Combat."

Sera looks at me as if I've gone mad. "You can't be serious. He'll kill you!"

I calmly say, "You're right. He'll probably best me." The word "best" is a gentle way of saying my demise will most likely be brutal and excruciating.

"I'm sorry, I shouldn't have said that."

I look at her like a daughter, this wonderful soul who could have been an apprentice and a fine arcanist. "I'm not upset. You had every right to say that. Yes, I'll probably die. But what a death!" Then I think about the glory of it all, and it's no longer glorious. "Forget I said that."

Sera, though, has her own idea. "What if you speak to him? Offer a truce of some kind?"

"He mocked me when he was Lord Arnaut." Just the thought of his deception has my blood boiling. "He pretended the entire time, and no one knew! I should have seen through the illusion. I knew Mortimer Allagant from the University. He was a bully and a tyrant then, and he's worse now, but he's still the same ugly being beneath it all. How was I so blind?"

"If the queen couldn't see it, nor Lord Gilliam, nor any of the others, especially after spending so much time with him, how could you?"

"He sent me chasing my tail, and you with me. I fell for his treachery."

Sera, kindhearted Sera, is sweet unto the end. "You did everything right. I want you to know, Ellis, that I respect you and admire you. Even if your magic is imperfect, you're perfect to me."

This compassionate girl; I don't deserve her or her admiration. But I do feel moved, a warmth that spreads through my chest, rising up to my cheeks like a comforting sunrise. If I go to my grave knowing that one person cared about me, it'll be enough.

I smile sadly, trying not to think of this as my last few hours.

I hear footsteps. The clang of the bar being raised behind our cell door. The slow groan of metal.

It's time to face death head on.

* * *

TRIAL BY COMBAT is as old as arcanists themselves, written into the laws of kingdoms. It's the soul of the arcanist creed, *Circuem Arcanum. Circle of Magic.* To serve and protect all that surround us.

I've lived long, I've seen much.

At the end of the day, the question will always linger: what have I done?

More specifically, what have I done with the time I've been given?

What deeds will be recorded to account for Heronium Ellis Whitefoot?

Will the record reflect a succession of disasters? A trail of near misses? A wave of blunders?

Or will it be written that Ellis the Arcanist lived and died in service to the crown, to the good people of Warren, to humble souls like Sera of Saplinger?

I would prefer the latter.

Trial by Combat has a single but simple rule: you fight until one side surrenders or perishes. If an arcanist like Mortimer Allagant lays claim to the throne of a foreign country, the Chief Arcanist of the opposing side can demand a Trial by Combat and defend the kingdom against the usurper.

It's before first light, and I'm standing in the queen's personal chamber, near the top of the keep. Allagant had allowed Sera and me to transfer into Sir Gilliam's custody. Apparently, we're harmless. How kind of him to think so little of my abilities yet again. Outside, the waves pound the rocks mercilessly.

"Your Majesty," I say, down on one knee. "Allow me to do this."

"You will die and I will lose my kingdom, you realize that, don't you?"

She doesn't have to be so harsh, but I understand: she hasn't made peace with her surrender. She refuses to believe that Allagant will destroy the monarchy and take Ravenmore by force before laying waste to the remainder of the kingdom, until lords and ladies everywhere bend the knee.

Sir Gilliam, tried and true, loyal Sir Gilliam speaks on my behalf. "Your Majesty, we will be outnumbered in a few hours. We might control Isla Kay right now, but that will change. We can't hold off both a fleet and an army. Your ship has been destroyed, so the only means to flee is on land, by horseback. Even if we were to ride with the wind, even if we had done so yesterday when Mortimer revealed his true self, we would never have reached Ravenmore in time. The Althanian fleet would eclipse us, gain the element of surprise, and destroy our moored fleet. Then they'd lay siege to our capital from the water while the Althanian army marches on the city's gates. We have no time to muster the troops from the southlands. Ravenmore will fall, and the monarchy with it, even if the citadel were to hold out and dig in. It might withstand a siege for a couple of months, but eventually the city will run out of supplies. The stores will empty and the will of the people will falter. Don't let that happen. Allow Arcanist Whitefoot to represent his country and die honorably, if that is what's to become of him."

The queen turns to Sera. "What about you? Should I put my trust in your master?"

"No," Sera says, much to our collective shock. "We should all put our trust in Ellis the Brave."

Ellis the Brave.

I like the ring of that. Too bad it will be the last time I hear it.

The queen gives Sera the respect she deserves. "Then we shall let it be. Heronium Ellis Whitefoot, servant of the crown, rise."

I come to my feet, hands folded humbly.

"By the power vested in me as monarch of Warren, I hereby proclaim you Chief Arcanist. You may proceed with your Trial by Combat. May the gods grant you quick mercy."

It's the best I could hope for. I gladly accept my queen's proclamation. "Thank you, Your Majesty."

* * *

THE SUN IS PURPLE like the standard of the kingdom I'm about to defend.

I wait on the seawall as my rival works his way toward me in the early dawn. His fleet is behind him, gaining rapidly on our position. Already, his cavalry has reached our border, five-hundred strong. The bulk of the army will catch up by day's end as the fleet awaits the command to sail onward, to Ravenmore.

The queen and former king are with their respective retinues on either side of the narrow seawall, witnesses to what is about to transpire, but heeding a safe distance. Sera is somewhere among them, but I try not to seek her out. I want to remember how she saw me, a foolhardy magician turned brave for a brief glimpse of time.

Mortimer Allagant is wearing black and red, the colors of his new kingdom. He's surefooted as he approaches. The seawall is a solid block of mortared stones, flat and a dozen feet wide at its widest point, butted up against a cliff face on one side and a steep plunge to the rocks and a watery grave twenty feet below. The air is saturated with brine, my hair and beard wet with the spray of the sea. Will this be the last thing I smell?

Neither of us have our wands out, but that will change in a moment.

Allagant stops thirty paces from me. He's as calm as I've ever seen an arcanist, confident and without a concern in the world. He expects to make quick work of me. If that's how I go, then it ought to be fast.

"This is quite novel of you, Ellis, this decree of Trial by Combat. I was of the mind to deny you, but if I'm to restore the Order of Arcanum to its former glory and amass a new force of arcanists, they must adhere to our creed. If they're to do so, then I should set the example for them and lay to rest any doubt which arcanist is the grandest in all of history."

He's full of himself, much more than when he was a snobby student. Our professors, were they still alive, would be appalled to see their prodigy turn into such a monster.

"I will fight you under one condition," I say. "If I win, your army and fleet must turn around and head home. Also, Althania will be restored to its own kingdom, along with its Grand Council, but under a monarch chosen by the council. Anders will be jailed for his subterfuge and aid in the murder of Warren's Chief Arcanist. Warren will retain its independence and sovereignty, and a truce will be drawn between countries."

"That's more than one condition," Allagant says.

"It is, but I stand by what I said. Just say *aye* and we can get on with it."

"You already know my terms. I will subjugate your lands. No

mercy will be given to any opposition. I think my condition is much more appealing than yours." Several of the Althanian nobles laugh their agreement. It makes the lump in my stomach that much heavier. "Say *aye* and it's a deal, Ellis."

"Then the winner's respective demands will be honored, is that correct?"

"It is."

"Then I say aye."

Allagant smiles. "Aye."

We reach into our waistcoats and retrieve our wands. His glows red at the tip, even brighter than in the keep. My tip is white, not as brilliant as his, but still noteworthy in my mind.

I wish I could recount the teachings of my instructors, the lessons I've learned from my classes at the University, the small bits of knowledge I've gleaned over the decades. All of my experiences are bottled up inside me. I know my incantations, my wand movements, things I started to share with Sera. Things I will continue to share with her if I am able. I want to live to see the University reopen, for Sera to be accepted into their arcanist program, for her to do well in school, to graduate, to become a guild member, and to be happy and free.

It's a good wish.

"Are you ready, Ellis?"

I take one more breath of salty air, then give my nod. "I'm ready."

A flick of his wrist and the words, "*Jetsom Alia*," and his wand explodes with red fire.

I'm barely able to utter the defensive intonation of "*Avatha!*"

The fire wraps around me, fended off by an invisible protective bubble around my person. I feel the scorching heat. It's gone as fast as it struck. Another second, and I'd have been roasted. Curls of evaporating seawater rise from my skin. I'm too occupied with the miracle of being alive to notice Allagant step toward me and thrust his wand forward. No words this time, just a powerful jab of energy.

I'm knocked back onto the hard stone below me. The crowd on either side begins a vocal torrent. "Get up!" I think I hear. "Kill him!" I also hear.

Allagant advances, wand raised.

Damn, I know that posture.

I roll to the side, stopping just short of the seawall's edge. The rock is obliterated where I was just lying. I'm pelted with stone and fragments of mortar. I view the sea below, churning madly in a swell, waves crashing against the vertical rockface, calling to me with their siren's song.

"*Horinius!*" I cry out, and a column of water shoots into the air.

It arcs high above us. Allagant looks up, curious, but then he produces a protective barrier with his wand as the water crashes down. It strikes the arched barrier squarely, but splashes me too. I struggle to hold on to stone made slick. Allagant dismisses his invisible shield. He fixes his sights on me and aims his wand. I roll the other way. A thunderous crack and the seawall sheers off, falling into the sea. I stumble to my feet as the cacophonous crash merges with the pounding of waves.

"Still here?" Allagant is enjoying himself, taunting me into answering his ridiculous question.

I cough up water that I'd swallowed. "Yes, still."

"We don't have to do this. You can lay down your wand and surrender. I promise to spare your life. Just say the word."

I've been bullied enough over the years, told what to do, and looked down upon. I won't allow Mortimer Allagant to get the satisfaction of winning by default. I won't!

"Sorry, old chap, it's not going to be that easy."

He smirks. If I had to venture a guess, he was hoping I'd turn down his offer. "Let's fix that, shall we?" He utters a command and the red tip of his wand sends a ripple of energy toward me.

"*Azzah!*" I cry, deflecting the energy. It angles sharply to my left, rupturing the wall beside me and punching out a shower of stone that scours the side of my face. My skin screams in pain, but my wand is up and ready.

I try to seize the moment to conjure an incantation that will neutralize Allagant once and for all. It worked with the basilisk. Why not here?

"*Magnum eruptus!*"

The ground trembles, and for a moment, I think it's going to give way, but the trembling ceases abruptly and just a few pebbles wobble out of place.

Why didn't it work?

Because you're cursed, Ellis, that's why!

Allagant raises his wand again, smiling at my failure. "Let me show you how it's done."

I manage to conjure another protective bubble as Allagant unleashes against me. I expect it to be fire or a wave of energy, but there's a searing flash instead, accompanied by an intense zap. My eyes are open, but . . .

But . . .

I can't see!

My bubble dissolves. I'm disoriented by the blindness.

I turn left and knock headfirst into the cliff wall. Pain judders through me. I lose my grasp on my wand and it falls.

No, no, no!

I drop to my knees and begin a frantic search while sightless, trying to feel around for the familiar piece of wood. Why can't I see?

"That's the thing with lightning," I hear Allagant say, closer now, as he answers my question. "Hot enough to melt skin and bone, faster than any force known to man, a gift of the gods to those who dare wield it. Have you ever met an arcanist who could control lightning, Ellis? They're a rare breed. The rarest! Ruel could control it. I've seen him do it. No one else. No one except me. And now . . . well, there's just me, isn't there?"

I stop my search.

There's no point.

Without my wand, I'm finished.

I can't hear the jeers of the crowd, not even the waves below, nor the whistle of the wind. Time slows. There's a strange calm washing over me, and a realization.

I've lost the fight.

It was always fated to happen this way.

I was cursed from the beginning, and cursed in the end. Damned by the gods. What else is there to do now but vocalize my surrender and ask for a merciful death?

It's one last thing to say, one last breath to expel, one final moment alive.

The words leave my throat, but they're not the words I'd meant to say. They're . . .

. . . a spell!

But not just any spell.

My old friend, the windkeeper spell.

The spell that nearly destroyed a duchy. The spell that accompanies me fittingly in the end now.

My curse has come full circle. I willingly accept my doom.

Stone and mortar erupt around me and I'm ejected into the air—or so I think. The air caresses my face lovingly. The upward motion frees me; my journey to the other side has begun. Then a falling sensation, growing faster, a lurch in the stomach, the sound of the surf coming up to greet me.

What a beautiful way to say goodbye.

* * *

I SPUTTER AND COUGH.

Cough and cough some more.

The horrendous taste of salt, snot and water coming out of my nose and mouth. My ears are filled with water, my pores brimming with it, my eyes stinging like they've never stung before.

My body, though, is a continuous shock of searing, white pain.

Then it's over, and I'm gasping air, looking up at wheeling seabirds and hearing my name.

"Ellis!"

Scraped and waterlogged, I sit up in the wet silt. I'm sandwiched between two boulders getting lapped by the relentless tide.

I'm alive?

"Ellis Whitefoot!"

I know that voice. "Sir Gilliam," I say and then begin a coughing fit again.

His armor removed, he's in breeches, quite comical under other circumstances. Sera scrambles down the rocks and heads toward me. She and Sir Gilliam help me to my feet. Nothing's broken, but my body feels as if it was splintered into pieces and then hastily patched together.

Sera is breathless, panting, soaked, but laughing too, as if she'd caught the madness from the former king of Althania.

As if struck by lightning again, I'm catapulted back to the moment before I plunged into the sea. I manage one word: "Mortimer?"

Sir Gilliam starts to laugh. I can't fathom what could be so funny, especially considering the man has never showed any emotion. Sera's laughing, too, afflicted with the giggles. I start laughing, then quit to cough, only to laugh again. What is wrong with us?

Sir Gilliam composes himself first. He says, "I am pleased to announce that you, Ellis Whitefoot, have bested Mortimer Allagant in the Trial by Combat."

"I have?" It's such a strange thing to say, just as the action of this knight is so odd to behold. "Mortimer surrendered?"

Sera shakes her head, smile lost. "Not quite. It's not something you'd want to see."

That would mean . . .

Allagant's dead?

It seems so preposterous, that I have trouble thinking of anything else for a long moment. "What of the Althanian army? What of their fleet?"

Sir Gilliam says, "The Althanian nobles have agreed that a territory dispute is not worth the cost of bloodshed and the loss of lives. They're standing down and sending everyone home."

"Really!" I had expected them to dismiss my condition to withdraw and demand the queen uphold Allagant's demands.

"It's too soon to know how this will turn out, but rest assured, Ellis Whitefoot, that you have saved the day." Sir Gilliam offers me a hand to shake. "I would be honored."

We shake on it, but as soon as he puts pressure on my hand, I wince in pain. "Sorry," I say.

Sera asks, "Are you ready to get out of here?"

I look up the cliff behind me. Did I really fall from up there? "I think that's an excellent idea."

* * *

THE QUEEN IS HUMBLER than I've ever seen her, an unfamiliar sight for anyone in her kingdom, I would imagine. She's removed her rouge makeup and requested Sera and I meet her in her apartment in the keep, a private audience. I can see the actual freckles in her skin. Sir Gilliam is the only other person present. One of the Althanian nobles had bequeathed his ship to us as a gift and gesture of goodwill. We're to sail home to Ravenmore in the morning.

After making the arduous ascent to the tower, I was welcomed with raucous applause and cheers, and then helped to a bath of hot water, along with a scrubbing stone to scour my skin clean. Not as luxurious as my last bath, but it feels good not to be a sodden mess. With clean pants, shirt and waistcoat, I feel like my old self, albeit in a great deal of pain from the bruises I've incurred.

The queen peers at me as if she's never seen me before, looking at my face, my eyes—me as a person, not as a servant. "Ellis Whitefoot, I owe you an apology. I didn't believe you could do it, and it almost cost me my kingdom. For that, I'm sorry."

Is this the same queen who dared me to disappoint her when we first met? "Your Majesty, you're most kind, but—"

"I'm not finished." I wait for her to continue. "As such, I'd like to offer you the office of Chief Arcanist. Permanently, this time, if you will accept the offer."

Chief Arcanist? Me? Is this a jest?

Of course it's not a jest. This is the queen, not Ilven Gaisen or Borgess Copperton.

I bow my head with humility. Sera is watching me, moist-eyed. She's going to make this old sap cry, too.

"Your Majesty," I say, grasping the reality of this once-in-a-lifetime offer, "I would be honored to accept."

"Excellent," she says. "Your first duty will be to reopen the University and restore honor to your order. Gods willing, it needs it."

"As you wish, Your Majesty."

"One more thing," the queen says. "Sera of Saplinger."

Sera perks up and comes to attention. "Yes, Your Majesty."

"This country owes you a debt of gratitude. *I* owe you a debt of gratitude. As such, I want you to complete your apprenticeship. The University shall have you. I will see to it personally. That is, if you want the opportunity."

Sera bounces up and down on her feet, then stops when she realizes it's the queen she's standing in front of. "It would be my honor, Your Majesty."

"Superb!" The queen claps her hands, not quite ladylike, but there's no one else but us four, and I've already seen Sir Gilliam laugh, which surprised me, but this is much more unexpected. I like it. "That will be all."

* * *

SERA AND I WATCH the gulls cry over the keep as the sun breaches the horizon. Yesterday, we were looking at our demise and the start of a country's slavery under a power-mad villain. Today, we stand free, ready to begin our marvelous new journey together. I'm breathing as I've never breathed before, and it's beyond words.

Sera leans her head against my shoulder. "Would you do it all again if you had to?"

The sun shimmers gold, red and a hint of purple like the colors of both kingdoms. There isn't a cloud in the sky. It's going to be a glorious day.

"Why, I couldn't imagine it any other way."

AFTERWORD

WHEW, THAT WAS CLOSE!

Well, for Ellis and Sera.

I hope they make the best of their new opportunities. They certainly deserve it.

Thank you from the bottom of my heart for reading CURSED MAGIC. I had a blast writing it. I pen lots of serious fantasy, so it felt good to break out of my mold and do something fun with a touch of humor.

If you enjoy stories of magic and winged beasts (ahem, dragons), then I have a treat for you—a preview of my short story, UNTAMED.

Like CURSED MAGIC, UNTAMED is set in a faraway kingdom. It's about a girl and her dragon—well, the dragon she wishes she had.

Turn the page to find out more about UNTAMED and to read an excerpt.

PREVIEW: UNTAMED

Great warriors ride wyverns.

But a dragon?

Unthinkable!

Especially not the daughter of the king. At least that's what Lina's condescending brother says.

Besides, the dragons are gone, vanished from the land. Lina doesn't believe it. Her great-grandfather the king had ridden the mightiest dragon of all, Saunder the Great.

Why not her?

Lina uncovers the clues that lead her to the cave where the beast slumbers. Saunder awakens, furious. If Lina doesn't leave right away, he promises to torch her, granddaughter of the late king or not.

Lina hasn't come this far to give up.

She would prove her brother wrong . . . and all of the other pigheaded nobles.

But what can she offer a dragon?

How can she prove herself worthy?

You'll love this epic fantasy, because it will capture your heart.

The following excerpt is from UNTAMED, available in eBook format.

Take a peek . . .

A FANTASY SHORT STORY
UNTAMED
STEVE PANTAZIS

UNTAMED

THE WYVERN RIDERS soared high above the castle's spires under the late morning sun. Lina imagined herself saddled upon the back of a great steed, its webbed wings beating against the current with a whooshing snap. Her brother Kieran would be eligible for apprenticeship with the Knights of Erendell on his name day in two years, at the age of sixteen. She'd see her name day three years after that, but her father would never grant her the opportunity to become a rider. After all, he was king, and what proper lady rode upon the back of a wyvern? She would be held to the duties of court, like her mother. It wasn't fair. She huffed her discontentment.

"Stop doing that," Kieran said. "I'm trying to watch."

She stuck her tongue out at him.

"Do that again, and I'll tell Papa."

"Go ahead."

Papa stood dutifully next to them, moving his hands silently like a wizard waving his wand, as if conducting the procession above.

"I'm going to fly among them someday," Lina said.

"No, you're not," Kieran said. "You're going to marry and have a dozen brats."

"Am not!"

"Am too!"

"Stop it, both of you!" Papa drilled into them with his steel-blue eyes, settling the matter in an instant.

Lina tried to cover her smile as her brother brooded, but was unable to wipe the smug satisfaction from her face. He was a scoundrel, and for that, she plied with vigor at getting under his skin.

Nobles and guards gathered on the tops of the castle walls, while the commoners and soldiers crowded the parade field just beyond the castle's perimeter. The crowds cheered as the wyverns swooped, one after another, hurtling earthward and then flattening out over the plains before climbing again. Lina forgot her brother, captivated by the majestic creatures and their long barbed necks, powerful hairless bodies rippling with muscles, and enormous wings, beating rhythmically as if to war drums.

Someday, she thought. She dreamed of sailing atop her mighty steed, piercing the skies and the heavens themselves.

* * *

MEISTER THRINDOR WRINKLED HIS NOSE. "Dear child, how many times have I told you, it was King Andelor who fought the Myrians in the All War, not your grandfather?"

Lina was only half paying attention to the Meister, plotting her getaway later that afternoon with her friend, Sef, the cook's son, to go explore the sea caves. Sef was also eleven, and by the Law, was forbidden from associating with the ruling class, much less the king's daughter. Today, the fog would conceal their movement outside the castle's walls, and none would be the wiser.

"Child, are you listening?"

Lina broke out of her reverie. "But King Lalian rode the last dragon, didn't he? Saunder the Great!" Her excitement got the better of her. The Meister was an irritable old man, and did not take kindly to outbursts, especially from a young girl. His frown lines deepened.

The Meister, whose bushy eyebrows sprouted like thistle, shook his head in the exasperated way he always did. "I cannot understand this fixation of yours with flying serpents. A dignified lady has no business sniffing out the details of dragons, or wyverns. Yes, dragons are a part of history, but they are just that: history!"

"But if I'm to learn our history, why not all of it? Saunder was a great dragon, was he not?" Lina expected a backlash from the Meister, but he sighed wearily instead.

"'Great' means many things to many people. Dragons are not wyverns. They do not aspire to be ridden, nor tamed, nor befriended, nor loved. They are reclusive, and the more you know them, the more you realize how rude, selfish and petulant they are, especially the older they get. Saunder was already old by many accounts, and, as those who can attest to it, quite cantankerous."

"Why did Grandfather seek Saunder out then?"

"To prove that a dragon could be ridden, I suppose. It was widely regarded as foolish, but your grandfather insisted."

"What did Saunder look like?"

"Like any dragon: scaly and about thrice as large as the largest wyvern. But unlike a wyvern, who knows not the speech of men, Saunder could speak many tongues. That's how your grandfather was able to—how should I put it?—*negotiate* with the creature."

"Grandfather tamed Saunder, didn't he? It's how he kept the Myrians from attacking us before we built the Wall, wasn't it?"

"Yes, but—"

"And he died gloriously in battle, didn't he?"

The Meister rolled his eyes. "One would wish for such an extraordinary death, but your grandfather didn't die in battle, nor did he die gloriously. He died after drinking himself silly and falling from his horse. The fall broke his neck."

"Oh."

"Of course, you won't find that in the history books."

"Did Saunder die?"

"Heavens no! That blasted anathema lives on. Sleeping, I assume, and hopefully for the next few centuries so everyone can forget he exists." The Meister settled his woolen robes about him. "Now, if we're through with all this nonsense, I'd like to resume our lesson."

Lina was too excited to listen to the Meister go on about the kingdom's history. The wheels were already turning in her head, and she would get Sef to help her.

* * *

"ARE YOU PLUMB MAD?" Sef asked as they picked their way south among the jagged rocks along the shoreline of the Coral Sea. They were west of the castle and north of the bay where the kingdom's fleet weighed anchor. Craggy cliffs yawned above them and to their left, but much of the rock face was obscured by fog.

"I'm not mad," Lina said just before slipping on a wet rock. She caught herself and kept going. She was dressed in plain beige breeches and a simple wool smock, as unassuming as her friend's, and hardly ladylike. The scent of seawater saturated the misty air.

"He slumbers south of here."

"What makes you think that?"

"I've seen the maps in the old library. There are lots of caves, but they're too small for a dragon. The wyvern warrens are north of the harbor. The wyverns could easily fit in the caves over here, but you don't see any, do you?"

Sef paused and ran a hand through his wheat-colored hair. It sat like a pile of straw atop his freckled face. "I thought that was because the knights liked their wyverns close to the castle."

"I thought the same, but the wyverns probably smell old Saunder. Wyverns are afraid of dragons."

"I wouldn't be surprised if dragons ate them. People, too." Sef glanced up as if worried a dragon might swoop down and eat them at any moment. It put Lina on guard too, but if her grandfather had faced a dragon before, why not her?

The rocks gave way to pebbles and sand, and for Lina, unfamiliar territory. The cliffs grew taller and farther back from the shoreline.

"How much longer?" Sef asked. "Father will be furious if I'm late to help with supper."

"Just past that break, I think."

Lina led them across a small dune dotted with seagrass. When they passed the sheer edge of the cliff's wall, it carved inward in a semicircular depression perhaps a mile wide. Gulls hovered above a massive craggy maw in the middle that made the cliff face seem like it was howling.

"Is that it?" Sef asked.

"Hush," Lina said in a loud whisper. "You don't want to rouse him."

Sef quieted in earnest, and the pair made their way to the cavern opening. Its height was staggering, large enough to swallow the fleet's largest warship, mast and all. Lina imagined what else the cavern could accommodate. No wonder the wyverns steered clear. Perhaps the gulls were fearless. Or oblivious.

The pair climbed over scree and tumbled rocks and Lina saw that the cavern went deep. Water dripped continuously with a *plunk-plunk*, and white-brown droppings spattered the lip of the cave. Lina expected to see a mountain of bones within the cavern, picked clean, but all she saw was a collection of stalagmites and broken rocks scattered about.

"It's okay," she whispered as they ventured inside.

The gloom thickened, and the saltwater smell was replaced by damp stone. A few dozen paces in, the stretch of cave cut sharply to the right, exposing murky depths that made it difficult to see more than a few feet ahead. Lina felt her heartbeat thrum in her chest from the anticipation. Just a little farther perhaps; then they could turn back, admit they tried, and laugh it off.

They paused behind a large bolder. The gloom faded to black, but there was something . . .

"You hear that?" Sef whispered.

There was a deep flutter, like the bellows that fed the furnace the smithies used to smelt ore. "Is that—" *Something breathing?*

The fluttering stopped, and Lina's breath caught in her throat. She dared not move. A rumble grew from the darkness, a heavy grinding that echoed loudly; then a shuddering hiss, followed by the scratch of something grating against stone.

Sef whispered that they should go. She knew he was right, but she needed to know if old Saunder lay beyond.

"Just a moment longer."

But Sef was already retreating, making a ruckus in his wake. She turned to go too, but stopped when she caught the flicker from the corner of her eye. It was a tiny glow, like a pot on a campfire cooking in the distance. The glow widened and rose, five feet, then ten, until it was high up. From its center a rumbling ensued, a rumbling which slowly formed into an unearthly voice that vibrated in her ears.

"I know you're there."

She shrieked and bolted, chasing after Sef, not daring to look back or see if she was about to be cooked. She caught up to her friend outside the cave, and together they raced across the sand under the darkening sky, tripping and falling a number of times until they were clear and away from the scare of their lives.

*** END OF EXCERPT ***

Thank you for previewing this epic fantasy adventure. Head over to https://tinyurl.com/UntamedStory or scan the QR Code below for your copy today!

ABOUT THE AUTHOR

STEVE PANTAZIS is an award-winning author of fantasy and science fiction. He won the prestigious Writers of the Future award in 2015 and has gone on to publish a number of short stories in leading SF&F anthologies and magazines, including *Nature*, *Galaxy's Edge* and *IGMS*. When not writing (a rare occasion!), Steve creates extraordinary cuisine, exercises with vigor, and shares marvelous adventures with the love of his life. Originally from the Big Apple, he now calls Southern California home.

You can learn more about him at www.StevePantazis.com.

ALSO BY STEVE PANTAZIS

Current and forthcoming short stories and novellas:

A Matter of Time

Aliens Anonymous

Apostate

Before I Let You Go

Between a Rock and a Fireball

C'est la vie, Humans

Chameleon

Cold as Space

Curse of the Goddess of Kaanapali

Daddy's Girl

Daughter of Time

Decadent Deception

Earth for Sale (Sold!)

Eternity's Traveler

Gods of War

Hex

Honor Bound

Humanity's Last Hope

I Dream of Stars

Illusions

In a Blink

In Darkness Lies

Infernally Yours

It's Only Skin Deep, Darling

Light in the Shadow of Worlds

Magic in the Land of Oppression

Murder on Moonbase 9

Odin's Daughter

Out of Print
Race to the Relic
Purple Orchid Eater
Reset
Surrogate
Switch
The Abernacle
The Daughter You've Always Wanted
The Devil Walks into a Bar
The Hunt
The Legacy
The Longest Mile
The Old Man and the Sea Siren
The Sacrifice
To Be Human
Universal Problem
Unlucky

CONNECT WITH STEVE

Get a **FREE eBook** just by signing up for Steve's newsletter: https://www.stevepantazis.com/join2

Support Steve at **Patreon** and receive early access to his short stories and novel chapters, along with cool swag: https://www.patreon.com/StevePantazis

To find out more about Steve and his happenings, check out these links:

Facebook page: http://facebook.com/SFFAuthor
Twitter: https://twitter.com/pantazis
Website: https://www.stevepantazis.com